8/24

# BIGGER THAN TEXAS

# BIGGER THAN TEXAS

## William R. Cox

GUNSMOKE

First published in the UK by Muller

This hardback edition 2009
by BBC Audiobooks Ltd
by arrangement with
Golden West Literary Agency

ISBN 978 1 405 68272 5

**British Library Cataloguing in Publication Data available.**

Printed and bound in Great Britain by
CPI Antony Rowe, Chippenham and Eastbourne

**William R. Cox** was born in Peapack, New Jersey. His early career was in newspaper journalism. In the late 1930s he began writing sports, crime, and adventure stories for the magazine market, and he made his debut as a Western writer with "Night of the Blood Bucket Raid" in *Dime Western* in the January, 1941 issue. It is worth noting that his Western story debut was with the first of several stories to feature a series character, Terry Glenn. During the 1940s Cox created a number of other series characters for the magazine market, most notably the Whistler Kid who appeared regularly in *10 Story Western* and Duke Bagley whose adventures usually were featured in *Star Western*. "The short story form was blissful until there were no markets," he once recalled. In the 1950s and 1960s Cox turned to television and wrote at least a hundred teleplays for such series as "Broken Arrow," "Dick Powell's Zane Grey Theater," "The Virginian," and "Bonanza." He also won a host of readers writing original paperback Western novels, the best known of which are novels about the adventures of two series characters originally published by Fawcett Gold Medal: Cemetery Jones in a series published under his own byline and the Tom Buchanan series which appeared under the house name, Jonas Ward. Dale L. Walker in the second edition of *Twentieth Century Western Writers* (1991) commented that William R. Cox's Western "novels are noted for their 'page-turner' pace, realistic dialogue, and frequent Colt-and-Winchester gun play. The series of novels built around the strong West Texas character, Tom Buchanan, are very typical Cox Western." Among his non-series Western novels, his most notable titles are *Comanche Moon* (1959), *The Gunsharp* (1965), and *Moon at Cobre* (1969).

# chapter one

THE TWENTY-ONE steers plodded, head down, through the snow-covered street of Field City. Johnny Bracket rode behind them, hat brim drooping. It was a good-sized town, one of the busiest in the Territory, but this night it was silent and the steady wind made a moaning sound through leafless trees.

There was a light at the livery stable. Johnny fell off his saddle onto feet numb from cold. His wiry bay pony nickered softly. A man opened the stable door and looked out, a small man with red hair and the beginning of a red winter beard. A sign said that Amsy Buchanan ran the place.

Johnny identified himself as he led the bay into the humid semi-warmth of the big barn-like structure. He asked, "You got a pen for the beef?"

"Pretty sorry, ain't they?"

"They're all that's left. They're breeders," said Johnny.

Buchanan nodded. There was a light of respect in his eyes.

"Reckon there was more of 'em when you left Texas."

He helped with the unsaddling and Johnny could feel circulation returning to his extremities as he moved slowly at the small tasks of arranging the bedding, wiping down the bay.

"Yep."

"Bad year, if a man got started late."

"Hell, high water, tick and the pestilence," Johnny told him. "Lucky to get those stockers through."

"You know where you are?" Buchanan surveyed him with speculative gaze.

"Yep."

"No land around here's any good except Morg Field land."

"I heard."

"Seems like he come from Texas, years back."

"I wouldn't know."

7

"Then you ain't a friend of his?"

"Never met the man."

Buchanan debated with himself, went to the door, closed it, returned to stare at Johnny again. "It'd be a right smart stunt if some lawman run twenty-odd steer in here, pretendin' to be a broke-down rancher."

Johnny asked wonderingly, "Now, why should a badge wearer be spookin' around Field City?"

Buchanan sighed, seemed to lose interest. "There's a pen out back. You're welcome to use it—nobody else will, not this time of year. Be a dollar for the pony."

There was four hundred dollars in the money belt, maybe twenty loose in his pants. It wasn't enough for the business he had planned, but at least he wasn't broke. He paid the man and went out on the street, conscious that Buchanan was disappointed in him, too cold and weary to wonder why.

The only other light was shining from a saloon called The Four Aces. He plodded down a boarded walk slippery under the snow. His jeans were greasy and dirty and his craggy young face sore with frost bite. His grey eyes were slightly sick with the miles he had come, but his shoulders were squared.

The Four Aces reeked with the odor of drying clothes, wet leather and unwashed men. He stood blinking in the lamplight, then moved past the cherry-red stove to the bar. He shook water from the flop-brim hat which he meant to replace on the morrow, then hung it on a peg and gestured at the stout bartender, a greasy-haired man.

Bottle and glass appeared, but the man held them until Johnny flipped a coin on the mahogany. It was a fancy saloon for a frontier town, with a long mirror and a painting of an overdeveloped naked lady. Johnny poured, turned, looked.

The men of Field City seemed no different from others he had seen between here and Texas. Most were concentrating on a poker game which was set up in a far corner.

A woman sat in the other corner at a large, round table. She was alone. Her glance swept over Johnny with unconcern, returned to contemplation of the game from afar. She was dark as the night without, and her eyes were larger than need be, Johnny thought, but she was a beautiful woman, younger than she appeared at first sight. Saloon girls were like that very often and he always felt a little sorry for them, even when he was using them. He was about to go toward this one when she turned the large brown eyes on him once more. They were like warning beacons, stopping him in his tracks.

A one-man woman, he thought, being kept by someone present in The Four Aces. Well, that was another matter. Later, maybe, after he found out how well she was being kept and by whom, something might be arranged. She was very lovely, part Indian, perhaps. Something about her rang a bell with Johnny Bracket.

He turned back to the bar; the bottle had been removed. He rapped a sore knuckle. The barkeep said, "That'll be another two bits."

Johnny grinned. There had been an awful lot of hard luck, about which he would not complain, and a terrible lot of lonely nights and tough going. It was nice to be able to have something at which he could strike back. "I gave you four bits the first time."

"Like hell you did."

The grin grew wider. "Now, bub, you wouldn't be callin' me a liar, would you?"

"Ain't you callin' me a liar?" The barkeep bristled like a small dog grown fat and feisty.

"Well, that's a hoss of an entirely different color," said Johnny in his softest Texan voice. "You *are* a liar."

As he spoke he stepped back from the bar. His Colt hung medium low and was tied around the worn jeans with a leather thong. His arms and legs were long and strong and when he looked at the barkeep as he did, grinning, he seemed to grow a bit in all directions.

There was an embarrassed silence as small dog reverted to type. The bottle and glass tinkled, reappearing. The bartender said, "Uh—well . . . maybe you're right about the four bits, at that. Man can make a mistake."

Johnny seemed a bit disappointed. "You pretty sure you are a liar, then?"

"A mistake." The bartender retreated, leaving the bottle and the shot glass.

"A liar," said Johnny.

Again there was a pause. Johnny moved a step. The bartender said quickly, "Okay, okay. Have it your way."

Johnny poured the shot glass full, all four ounces. He said, "Thanks, bub. I really didn't want to turn loose." He carried the whiskey over to the poker game and stood, watching. Behind him the girl's big eyes narrowed for just a moment on his back, then swiveled to the big man sitting at the poker table whom she had been watching all evening as her mind went around and around in a circle, getting no place.

The big man was Morgan Field, it quickly developed, whom his friends called "Morg" rather more often than necessary. The city was named for him. Johnny marked him in his mind, a florid man, all solid beef, with a thick neck and a quick eye. His eyes were set rather far apart and the brows slanted downward at the outer edges, lion-like. He had long fingers, very white, slender, out of proportion to the rest of him. His lower jaw protruded just a bit, not enough to be ugly.

Next to Field was a fattish man. Johnny's memory flickered, he knew the fellow. Someone called him "Calhoun" but that was not the name. He tried to bring it all into line, remembering El Paso when he had been just a button looking for a job, playing a little poker to keep alive, milking the saloon games for eating money.

That was after his mother had died. The figure of Joe, his tall, leathery father impinged on the scene. It had been years since he'd seen Joe Bracket or either of his two brothers. Joe still had the small spread but it wasn't home any more. For a moment he was homesick, then he remembered the last hot quarrel and his abrupt leave-taking and the woman Joe had married, a young woman, good-looking, nothing wrong with her except she wasn't Ma.

Sam and Toole had already left the place. Sam was the eldest Bracket boy, a marshal in Farwell, a fast gun, a smooth man, always in the money. Toole was an adventurer, smart as a whip, some said not above a quick holdup or bank robbery, but also sometimes an undercover man for Wells Fargo, Johnny knew.

They were all doing fine but Johnny. This had been his chance and a series of bad breaks had ruined it. He had the money in his belt and he had those twenty-one steers and his gun and the bay, but he had no place called home.

He snapped back to El Paso and then he had it. "Callahan" was the name. The man had been much thinner and quicker. He could see the broken veins caused by heavy, now daily doses of booze; he could see the blinking eyelids. Yes, it was Callahan, all right, and very interesting it could be to meet him here.

Next to Callahan-Calhoun sat an elderly fellow with whiskers and the far-away expression of the prospector the world over. He had a straight nose and a leathery aspect and he didn't say much, but the others called him "Lonely."

Alongside Lonely was an Englishman with the clipped accent of his breed, a medium-sized man also showing the signs of alcoholism. His skin was pink and baby-like and he was a loser in the game and a bad poker player at that, Johnny perceived in the space of a couple of pots.

The other player was the town law, his badge pinned to a woolen shirt beneath a leather vest and his name proved to be Mulloy. There was room for another chair. The onlookers, odds and ends of townsmen and three riders who stood against a wall together, stared critically as Johnny pulled up a chair and raised an eyebrow at Morgan Field.

"Name of Bracket. Mind if I squat?"

Field hesitated. His stare was comprehensive, going over the worn range outfit to the money belt Johnny was unbuckling, then to the gun in its open holster, then to Johnny's countenance. Nobody spoke, awaiting Field's decision.

The man had a big, booming voice. "Sure, Bracket. Anybody with money to buy in is welcome."

Johnny stacked the worn bills. It was Mulloy's deal, which put him under the gun and he passed after a cursory glance at a busted flush. Mulloy was thin-faced, hard-bitten, about Field's age, in his mid-thirties.

From the looks of things, Callahan-Calhoun was the big winner, the prospector, the Englishman and Mulloy the losers, Field neither far up nor far down. Mulloy dealt the requests for cards with painstaking, slow care. He had blunt fingers, stubby, not clever.

Field won a small pot and it was Johnny's deal. He worked the stiffness out of his hands and managed to shuffle without dropping the deck. Mulloy cut and the cards went around. Field opened carelessly for two dollars.

Calhoun-Callahan was staring at Johnny. He shook his head as though to clear his mind and played along for the two buck bet.

Lonely found players and Monty, the Englishman, hesitated, obviously low in funds, then he also stayed. Mulloy said harshly, in a rasping, annoying voice, "Driver's seat rises and raises."

He put in ten dollars. Johnny looked at his cards. He had

two aces and a pair of treys. Without hesitation he called the raise. He was in the best position to estimate the other hands, he had two or three ways to make a play.

Field met the bet, saying in his loud, confident fashion, "Now it gets interestin'. Maybe you brought life into it, Bracket."

"Maybe I'm buyin' trouble," said Johnny, watching Calhoun-Callahan. The fat man counted out eight dollars with meticulous care. Lonely dropped.

The Englishman fingered his money, looked at the ceiling, and threw in his cards. The stove gave off good heat but not enough to make him sweat so much, Johnny thought.

"Cards, if any," Johnny said, laying down his own five smartly edged, a coin atop them.

"Three," said Field.

Johnny dealt the three, aware that Field had only played in the pot because he was rich and bored, not underestimating the man.

"Two here," croaked Calhoun-Callahan.

Mulloy stood pat, thereby posing a perplexing decision for Johnny. He looked around the table, edging out his original five cards. He thought deeply. Against anything but a pat hand he would have discarded the treys. Against a possible bluff, or if he knew the players, he might have stood pat and raised. Now, he thought, he was trapped with a weak hand after the draw and had to better it. There was really only one thing he could do.

"One to the dealer," he stated flatly. He felt Mulloy move beside him and imagined the lawman was holding a straight. He wondered now about the fat gambler across the table. He watched him very closely.

Field said, "Opener checks."

"Check to raise," said Calhoun-Callahan.

Mulloy was ready, surmising he would have to bet them. "Ten dollars."

Johnny had not peeked at his draw. He said, "And fifty."

Field laughed. "That's the way to bet 'em, Texas."

Calhoun was shuffling the five cards, again staring hard at Johnny. Finally he said, "No bet."

Mulloy was now doing a bit of sweating on his own. Fifty dollars was a big bet, especially into a pat hand. Still, Johnny hadn't looked . . . his straight should be the winning hand. And if it was the winning hand, he should raise another fifty back into Johnny's teeth. On the other side, if Johnny was one of those wild men who played a four flush as though he had it made . . . he may have made it, in which case the straight was no good. Mulloy's mind was not quick, but it was thorough. His trouble was that he had never been a very good poker player.

He said, "Call, damn it."

Johnny dealt the cards face up, ace, ace, three, three . . . and another three. "Well, what do you know? I filled."

He took in the money. Field roared with amusement. "You got the look of a man that's been fresh outa luck. Maybe you busted the streak, huh, Texas?"

"Johnny Bracket," he said. "Men that get called 'Texas' generally don't pull their weight, somehow or other."

"Gimme the cards, Johnny, and let's have a real game."

The big man dealt with dexterity, but his hands were honest enough. Monty looked hungrily at Johnny, as if wishing he could borrow some luck. Lonely just sat, saying nothing. Mulloy tapped the table, angry at himself for losing the pot, yet knowing that he had been helpless against a lucky draw, disliking Johnny for having been the instrument of defeat. It was like almost any other poker game up and down the western frontier except for one factor . . . Calhoun-Callahan.

When the fat gambler opened for five dollars, Johnny thought he felt the building of it. Lonely played, so did Monty, without his usual hesitation. Mulloy couldn't wait to get his money in.

A cold deck? Johnny wondered. He thought he would have detected a run-in, but sad experience in the past bade him beware. He looked at his cards. He had a pair of tens. It probably was not a cold deck because six hands are as easy to set up as five. He folded, shaking his head. He sat back in his chair, watching from beneath lowered lids.

Field raised ten dollars. Everybody played. It was, Johnny thought, just one of those pots, as he had first intuitively suspected. Poker is an exciting game because of such go-arounds, when everybody is holding good cards.

Calhoun-Callahan took two cards. Lonely took one. Monty took one, Mulloy did likewise. Field dealt himself two.

El Paso, thought Johnny, years back. Harry Hatt, the gambling fool who was shot by one of the Duke twins, was in the game, both the Dukes and another man. From the sidelines it had been easy to see the play. Nobody had caught on, either, and Johnny had known better than to open his mouth, him an unknown kid without a gun on him among those hot shots.

Now Calhoun-Callahan had dirty shirt-cuffs, flaring wide, and the sleeves of his coat were built loose. It was an ill-lighted room and the players were intent upon their cards.

The fat man said, "My turn to bet fifty."

Lonely tipped money into the pot with a horny, curved forefinger. Monty swallowed hard, then put his last bills into the pot. Mulloy choked, picked up a wad.

"I raise fifty."

Field said, "I, God, I'll raise another fifty."

Calhoun-Callahan had added a lot of weight since El Paso. He had lost other things, thought Johnny. He wasn't so fast. Maybe his nerve was gone. His fingers shook just a little as he went for a hundred dollars to re-raise the pot. Johnny imperceptibly cleared his chair.

Lonely was looking at his cards, inscrutable behind his grey whiskers. He finally shook his head and deposited his cards in the center of the table. Monty gasped, then followed suit.

Field said, "And fifty to you, gambler."

The fat man said, "And a hundred more, Morg."

Mulloy said, "I'm in the middle, damn it." But he saw the raises.

"And I'm bettin' into the raise," Field said, laughing, not caring very much. "I call you, gambler."

Calhoun-Callahan laid them down. "Four fat ones."

The four aces caught the light, reflecting it. The fat man made a subtle move while the others gaped. Johnny went clear across the table.

He pinned the thick wrist. He twisted hard and a hold-out slid clumsily out of the frayed, dirty cuff. From it fell Calhoun-Callahan's original hand, five unmatched, useless cards.

"Better count the deck, gents," said Johnny.

There were exclamations, curses, cries of amazement. Chairs crashed, men milled. Johnny held tight to the wrist, looking down at the cornered gambler, feeling a little sick, a little sorry at what he saw in the agonized eyes.

"I, God," roared Morgan Field. "We been nursin' a viper. Empty his damn pockets, Mulloy. Split his take back accordin' to who put in what. Then stick him in the hoosegow and let him rot."

Johnny was watching the eyes, set deep in fat but glowing like coals. "You should know better, Callahan. You lost your quick some place."

He meant it as a warning. He had to let go and slide back across the table and he sensed the rat coming out in the fat man and he didn't want the trouble. Even as he moved he knew the message did not get through, that Calhoun-Callahan had passed the line of reason and was hell bent. Perhaps he had been in western jails before, perhaps he knew Morg Field's jail would be worse than most.

The fat man's derringer was up the other sleeve. It came out with very nice speed. Men fell away yelling. It was a nasty little double-barrelled gun that would make a terrible hole at close quarters.

Johnny side-stepped as he cleared the Colt. The derringer went off and men dived for the floor. It was necessary to be very careful lest a bystander be hurt.

Johnny aimed, then pulled the trigger. Calhoun-Callahan's head jerked, his face vanished beneath a mask of sudden blood. He went to his back on the floor, dead before his body struck and the silence in the room was profound.

The woman in the corner had not stirred, Johnny noted. There was a wine glass in front of her. She raised it, looked at him as she sipped, but gave no further sign.

## chapter two

MORGAN FIELD led the way to the table in the corner. The girl looked up at Johnny and he was sure now that she had Indian blood, probably Navajo, because of the slant of her brows, her coloring and the control she continued to show.

"Johnny Bracket, this here is Susan Carter."

"An honor, Miss."

She nodded and again raised the wine glass, not speaking. Field sat down beside her, sprawling, motioned to the barkeep. "Calhoun's been around, not winnin' much, for a month. Reckon you about saved us from a good trimmin'. You say you recognized him? From where?"

"El Paso," said Johnny. "Years back."

"You an El Paso boy?"

"No. I was young and hungry."

"Didn't know anybody down there?"

"Got to know Harry Hatt and the Duke boys later on."

"The twins?" Morg Field chuckled. "I mind the twins, all right. No wonder you play a good hand of poker."

"Never worked at it. I'm a cattleman."

"I see." The bottle appeared, a special one with a label. The whiskey was aromatic. The girl drank wine from a carafe. The surly barkeep was all fawning smiles and useless little brushing gestures.

Johnny said, "Got twenty-one stockers left, down at the stable. Got about five hundred dollars. You know where I can lease with option to buy?"

"You know who I am?" asked the big man.

"It's your town. Field City."

"I, God, it is, at that. Had less than you got when I came here. This was supposed to be minin' country. I brought in the first steer."

"Sure. I heard."

"You got any special reason for comin' here?"

Johnny's cracked hands lay on the table. He turned them up, showing the calluses. The heat was irritating them. "Where else would I go?"

"That's right. Must've been rough, gettin' here."

"Late start, bad ending."

There was a small silence. The girl was looking past him, at where the men were still doing what had to be done for Calhoun-Callahan. There was a bumping sound as they staggered, hitting the door jamb as they carried him out on a shutter, but the girl's expression did not change.

Morgan Field said, "You need more'n a lease. You need land you got title to."

"I'm a few thousand short of cash."

"And I'm a banker. I lend money and get back interest," said Field. "What you need is credit."

"Take the cash and let the credit go, my Pa always says. But then, Pa never was much of a businessman."

"Credit. That's the secret. My bank lends on a man's head and it don't foreclose unless the man goes bad. We need

cattlemen around here. I like Texans with guts. So . . .
there's the Jenkins place."

Johnny sipped the good whiskey. "Mr. Field, let's get
something straight. Right now I had to kill a man. That
ain't my way to go. It just happened. Only other man I
ever shot was a horse thief. I don't like shooting people."

"I need a killer, I hire him," said Field. His eyes shifted
and he grinned faintly, without mirth.

The three riders he had noted earlier, Johnny saw, following Field's glance, were still against the wall. They had
made no move to help with the dead gambler. They stood hip-
shot and at ease, drinking beer out of bottles, only now they
twisted torsos so that they faced toward the corner table.

"My boys. They work the ranch. Rag Shade, Goober Halliday and Arnie Frey. Top hands, but they ain't much at
handling cattle," said Field. "They would've blasted Calhoun
all to hell and gone if he'd pointed that derringer at me."

Johnny nodded. "Like I say. It's your town."

"My Circle F runs north of the Jenkins place to the Padre
range. Tom Mulloy's got some beef grazes the lower pastures,
you and him can make a deal with your stockers. There's
enough pasture if everybody agrees to get along. Man with
guts could get rich in five, ten years."

"What's the deal?" asked Johnny.

"The house needs work. Bein' wintertime, you can rebuild. Fences, barns, everything got run down. The bank
loans the cash, takes back a mortgage of five thousand dollars. That's to buy more cattle, get you started good."

"It's mighty generous," said Johnny.

"No country's any good without manpower. The right
kind. I ain't Santy Claus. I'm a businessman. You want
land, I'll give you the chance to own it."

Johnny said, "Why, if it's a business deal and you think
I'm good for it, then I'll be grateful."

"The winters are hard here but we can survive 'em. It's
rail end here, the cattle weighs out, we get the best price.
We work together here in the country. Cuts costs." He waved
a big hand, grinned. "Tonight you can sleep at the hotel, just
mention my name. The Chink'll rustle you a bath, you can
see the barber tomorrow. Them hands need attention.
Noonish, you and me can take dinner. Okay?"

Johnny recognized dismissal. He didn't blame the **big**

man; Susan Carter was the best looking woman he had seen in many a moon. He got up and said, "Okay. Thanks."

"Don't thank me, thank Calhoun."

"His name was Callahan in El Paso," said Johnny. "Maybe they better put both names on the headboard."

He bowed to the girl in the best Bracket manner—all the men in the family were woman-conscious, woman-wise. He wrapped his sheepskin-lined coat around him and went out into the frigid night.

Morgan Field leaned back, looking around the room. He caught Tom Mulloy's eye and beckoned to him. The Marshal came to the table with some money and a wallet. He sat down and Field poured whiskey for him.

"Miss Carter," said Mulloy, nodding to the girl. He pushed the money toward Field. "Too bad the Texas dude had to spoil it. There ain't much profit, way it is now."

"The fat man was too dumb. We couldn't have used him much longer. Booze got him down."

"It was a good idea, though. One of your best. We coulda milked the town."

Field shrugged. "There'll be another tinhorn along one of these days."

Mulloy asked, "What about the Texan?"

"You ever know any Brackets around El Paso?"

Mulloy thought a moment, his brow deeply furrowed. Then he said, "I'd know if there was a family—a ranch—anything like that. Can't remember any."

"After our time. That's what I thought. But check it out, Tom. I'm putting him on the Jenkins place."

Mulloy's face darkened. He protested, "A stranger next door to me? I dunno about that."

"You had Jenkins, he wasn't a stranger."

"The double-crossin' bastard!" Mulloy spread his hands. "Yeah, I guess. If we watch him."

"We help him, Tom. We let him build. You know that breed. Quick gun, strong back, weak mind. They work outa pride and ambition. He'll build an operation we'll be happy to own . . . when we want to take it."

"Guess I'm too cautious," said Mulloy. "I always figure on bein' plenty careful."

"Careful didn't get me where I am," said Field flatly, with pride. "I, God, this Territory is about all of it going to be mine, or close enough to me to be like my own. It only takes brains and guts and ambition. You only got to know what you want and to look ahead a bit."

"And hire the right people," said Mulloy.

"Not you, Tom. You ain't no hired hand. You come up with me and you're going to stay with me." Field's voice was warm and friendly.

"We sure come a ways together."

"You durn betcha we did. Now, you wanta go and start telegraphin' about that Texan?"

"I sure do." He finished his drink. "Miss Carter." He bowed stiffly as he departed. The girl looked after him with complete indifference.

Field asked, "What do you think, Susan?"

Her voice was surprisingly light and tinkling, like music. "The Texan, yes. Tom, as I've often said, absolutely no."

"He did miss it with the gambler. He should have butted in there, stopped Bracket from killing him. But Tom goes away back. That gun of his saved me more'n once."

"Back-shooting," she said.

"I wasn't particular."

She finished her drink. "Yes. That's probably it."

He frowned at her. "I'm not about to kill anybody. Never. Don't ever worry about that."

"No. You won't kill anybody."

Rare unease stirred him. "Nobody will ever get anything on me. I can't afford it. I know it."

She said, "I understand."

"You're safe, you know that, too."

She didn't reply, turning the glass around in her shapely, brown hands.

He said, "You and me, we make a team."

Still she did not answer him, her eyes going across the barroom to a table where Lonely Jones sat with Monty.

"All right, we can't get married. You knew that all along." His voice was low, brutal.

"I knew it. That doesn't make it any easier."

"You got to be tough, Susan. That's what got you here, with money in the bank and diamonds in your bureau drawer."

"I'm tough."

He sloshed a good four fingers of whiskey into his glass and downed it. "Mebbe you better go upstairs. See you in a little while."

She arose obediently, not looking at anyone in the room, walking slowly, with catlike grace, to the door through which she had entered. He heard her heels clicking on the steps leading to the upstairs apartment he had built when he brought Susan to Field City. The unease stayed with him. It was not pleasant to think that something had to be done about the girl. He was very fond of her.

He had caught her picking his pocket in a clip joint on the Barbary Coast when on one of his San Francisco flings. She was ragged and filthy but she spoke better English than he. She had been convent-educated at the behest of her Yankee father, who had then wandered off, leaving her Navajo mother to die of privation. The rest was a common story, laudanum and liquor had completely debauched her. There was a dark streak in her but he had been able to clean her up and beat her into subjugation in a remarkably short time. Once off the drugs and alcohol her recovery had been amazing.

The trouble was, it had worked too good. He stared at nothing, thinking about it. Even while he had been whipping her to make her give up the drugs, he had sensed it. She began by hating him and in a week she was his slave.

Now she was unhappy because they could not be married lest her past be discovered—she had been well known in San Francisco because of her wild delinquency. No matter what she said or did, she would remain discontented. He had to think of some way to manage without hurting her.

Maybe a house, he thought, and this pleased him. She was possibly too temperamental to make a good madame, but Field City was growing and he could keep an eye on her. The more he thought about it the better he liked it. He could keep a small percentage just to maintain the link between them. After all, he had found her in a house. She couldn't complain that she had lost position in the world.

Or, rather, she would complain but he would overwhelm her with his logic. The main thing was to do the best for her without hurting her and without endangering himself.

There had been enough danger all down the line since El Paso. It was a hard country and a man had to do certain things to stay on top. He had fought his way to the peak of the dunghill and he intended to go farther and find other hills to scale.

He got up and crossed the room, a graceful, full-bodied

man weighing over two hundred pounds. He did not crook his finger at Lonely Jones, he knew better than that. He went to where the prospector sat and raised an eyebrow at Monty, who was drinking himself into his Saturday's shadows.

"Lonely."

"Morg." The old man did not ask him to sit down, but he took a chair and the barkeep trotted over with the whiskey bottle and a glass, then poured for the three of them. Monty muttered something but the others paid no attention.

"How is Mary?" asked Field.

"Okay."

The silence deepened as they drank sparingly and Monty seemed to go asleep sitting upright on the hard chair, his white, useless hands folded around his glass of liquor.

"Thought any on the proposition I made you?" Field asked.

From behind the full growth of whiskers Lonely said, "Nope."

In the most kindly fashion, Field said, "You been traipsin' the mountains for forty years and what have you got to show for it, Lonely? A house and lot. Enough to feed you and Mary, just barely. It's time you quit and came home and took care of the girl and the place."

Lonely's mild blue eyes were upon the somnolent Monty. His voice barely reached Field. "Come off it, Morg."

"No, I'm serious. The bank can use a man with your long residence and experience. New people are comin' in all the time. You'd be a good one to talk to them."

"Come off it."

"Why, your own son, Mary's father, founded this town. You could be one of the biggest men in the Territory if you'd consider my deal."

"You're the big man, Morg."

"Well, sure. I earned it."

"You're smart."

"I studied things out."

"You run things your way."

"For the good of Field City, you know that."

Lonely turned and looked him in the face. "You're a goddam liar, a thief and a bully, Morg. What the hell is the use of comin' around me and Mary and makin' out otherwise?"

Field laughed. "Damned if you ain't a case, Lonely."

"Yep. I'm a case."

"Mary don't run me off."

"Mary's got some of her pa's damn foolishness in her."

"So long as she'll see me, I'll be around."

"She's kinda soft, but she ain't *that* dumb. Better save your time and energy."

"If she marries me she'll be the richest woman in the Territory some day."

"If she marries you, she'll be dead within the year."

For a moment the anger was thick and black, then Field laughed again. "You are a case and a half, Lonely. Think it over now, seriously. I'll talk to you later."

He got up and went back past the table in the corner, paused and blew out the lamp on the wall. The barkeep came to him with a sack containing the night's receipts. The Four Aces Bar was about to close for the night.

Lonely Jones took Monty's arm. The two of them rose and went to the street door, Monty walking like a mechanical doll, but walking alone, not leaning on his older companion. The other customers strayed after them. Field walked to the door and watched.

"The old sonofabitch," he muttered. "He'll die off by himself in the hills; I won't have to do anything about him. The old sonofabitch."

He went through the door. On the stairs he could smell the scent of the woman who waited for him above. He hefted the sack, it was a good night's take despite the untimely killing. Business was always good in The Four Aces since he had managed to close two other places. Only the Mexican cantinas were running now, and of course they were necessary for the lower classes to foregather and drink.

The customers of those places had votes like anybody else and more of them.

He had learned a lot since Texas days. Lucky he could read. He could thank old Manny Freed for that, the outlaw who carried books in his saddlebag. It was Manny who had explained about the newspapers from the East and that by reading them a man could learn what was going on in the whole world. There wasn't another person in Field City who took the New York papers.

Yes, he had built well. It was a nice little town and it would be bigger and better. He was real proud of himself, his chest swelled as he went down the hall to the luxurious rooms which no one ever saw but Susan Carter, the cleaning woman and himself.

# chapter three

THE SUN STREAMED frostily through a window and fell across the bed. Johnny Bracket started out of his dreams with the guilty fear that he should have been on the road long since. Then he realized he was in a bed, a real bed, for the first time in months. It was a good room, with a high ceiling, at which he stared, luxuriating in the softness of a pillow filled with goose feathers.

First, the dream, in which his father had berated him as usual, repeating, "Anything you get for nothin' is worth what you pay for it."

True, he thought, but I paid for it by shooting old Callahan-Calhoun. That wasn't a thing I wanted to do, it was because he outed with his little gun and went to ventilate me. It just so happened that Morgan Field was in the game.

All right, he conceded to the wraith of his dream, maybe it was some kind of a dodge. Field was sharp enough. Maybe it wouldn't work out, but a man had to open the door when opportunity knocked. No sense to refuse an offer before investigating.

Killing Callahan-Calhoun was a misfortune but it had not disturbed his sleep. He had seen a lot of killing, and most of it didn't make as much sense as the death of the tinhorn.

He got up, shivered, washed hastily, rummaged in his warbag for decent clothing. He had a silken neckpiece, which he knotted carelessly. The barbershop would be open, and he wanted a warm bath more than anything in the world. Last night he had dabbed himself before entering between the clean sheets, but it wasn't the same as a tub.

The room was clean and the hallway was clean and even the carpeting on the steps was swept down. In the lobby there were several leather chairs and behind the desk was a small man with a withered arm who said his name was Cotton, and who was no more surly than desk clerks ever are. Johnny shrugged into his sheepskin and went out onto Main Street.

The air was fresh and bracing; his breath made a small cloud. The streets were clean, too, he saw. The buildings were four square and evenly spaced. Last night the town had been ghostly, this morning it was sharp in detail and interesting to a newcomer. There was a stone bank building and a brick general store and warehouse.

Strangest sight of all, there was a village square. It was in the middle of the town and all around it were buildings facing on it. The barber shop was at one corner.

Down the street, leading west from town, was the church, a white painted building, not very large, but with a real steeple. There was a lot more to Field City than he had expected, Johnny thought, heading for the striped pole which heralded his coming warm bath.

The barber's name was Simon Jarret. He was a tall, thin man, balding, sandy-haired, grey-eyed, sharp-nosed, with a wen on his right temple. There were two other citizens in the shop. One was Lonely Jones. The other was the livery stable man, Amsy Buchanan.

Jarret said, "Been expectin' you, Bracket. See you left off your gun, that's nice, shows good bringin' up. Sunday's no day to tote iron. You want a bath first or shave first? Either way's all right with me."

There was only one chair, beyond was a room which held a pool table and an old music-making machine, coin-operated. Bottles of soft drinks and beer were in a large pail which contained a floating piece of ice. Again Johnny was struck by the cleanliness of the establishment.

He said, "I believe I'll get rid of the Texas mud. Must be some in the crevices."

"Been expectin' you." Jarret had a voice which went on and on, not harsh, slightly mellifluous. "Morg was in earlier, said you'd be by. Been holdin' up Amsy, thought you wouldn't be much later than now."

Johnny said to the livery stable man, "I'm sorry."

"Oh, that's all right. Anything for one of Morg's men." The irony was smooth but certain.

For a minute, Johnny debated. He knew that Lonely was waiting for his answer, saw the question in the old prospector's faded blue eyes.

He said, "I reckon you people better get it straight. No Bracket ever wore any man's collar."

Jarret interjected with celerity. "Amsy's got a bug up his rump. Just don't pay no attention. The bath's that way."

There was a door and beyond it a room with a stove going. The reservoir was a wooden cask set high and reinforced with sturdy iron hoops. Pipes led into the cask and out, with faucets depending above a circular oaken tub.

Johnny turned on the tap and peeled off his clothing, hanging it carefully on hooks where the steam could worry out some of the wrinkles. He was long in the leg, his torso was ridged with muscle which now began to loosen from the rigors of his journey. He slid a cake of soap into the water. It was too hot, so he adjusted the cold water and let himself slowly down into the bath.

Amsy Buchanan, he thought, and certainly Lonely Jones, were not Field's people. In a town like this, a one-man shebang, there had to be rebels. However much good a man does, there are those who resent single-o.

But the town was orderly, laid out checkerboard, streets swept, garbage not aslop in public, people seemingly prosperous enough. Morg Field probably had a heavy hand, but the results were, at least to the eye, satisfactory.

And anyway, loaning from a bank was a business proposition; he wasn't beholden to Field. There was the mortgage, there would be years of hard work ahead. Lonesome work, too, he added. He wasn't a man who enjoyed being alone. All the Brackets liked to be among company, liked to talk and to listen.

He soaped his head and dug hooked fingers into his scalp. He found a brush and took off some skin around the ankles and knees and wrists. His hands were softening up pretty good but the harsh soap and hot water made them sting.

It might be interesting, he thought, people like Amsy Buchanan and Lonely Jones and whoever else taking a stand, putting democracy on trial. If Morg Field was right, there was plenty to go around. Cattle could winter here and grow fat before shipping time on spring and early summer grass. If there was any mining, Field City could become a center of operation. To be in on the ground floor of such a boom couldn't help but be rich-making.

The door to the bath opened and closed. He squinted past

soapy eyelids, dabbed at himself with a towel and said, "That you, Mr. Jones?"

"Umph." The prospector leaned against the wall, edging around to a position across from the portal through which he had entered.

"Be through in a minute."

"Take your time. Know how it feels, after so long a stretch." The voice was rusty like a seldom-used hinge.

"On the trail you get to dreamin' about it."

"Same way in the desert. Mountains, now, you get water."

Johnny ducked himself all the way under, then floated a bit in the tub, turning over, splashing. Then he pulled the stopper. He let cold water run over him, washing off the suds. He yelled mildly, slapping himself, then leaped over the side, grabbing a fresh towel, rubbing himself hard.

"Hear you're goin' to take over the Jenkins place," said Lonely.

"News gets around fast in Field City."

"Umph."

"Well, looks like I may, after I've seen it," said Johnny. "Field made me a good proposition."

"It's run-down."

"Field said it was."

"Got a notion."

"Okay, let's hear it."

"Monty," said Lonely. "Carruthers."

"The Britisher?"

Lonely nodded. "Before booze and America, he studied architecture. Engineerin'. Needs a start."

Johnny wiped one foot, then the other, put down the towel, stood on it, picked up his clean drawers. "I can't hardly stand a drunk, Mr. Jones."

"He's a drunk."

"Anyone could see it."

"Needs help."

Johnny pulled the wool-lined undershirt over his head. "Friend of yours?"

"Good man. Honest. Never tells a lie."

"Friend of yours?" Johnny repeated.

"Good friend," said Lonely firmly. "I'd give a pretty penny to see him get off the liquor."

"He want to get off it?"

"I dunno," said Lonely. "Needs the chance."

Johnny yanked at each leg of the pants, wished for an iron, stuck his legs into them, yanked them tight around his narrow waist. "You think he can help rebuild, is that it?"

"Figure you ain't a hand with a hammer and saw."

"That's bright figurin'," said Johnny ruefully.

"Most Texas cattle men can mend a fence is about all."

"That's me." He hesitated. There was something urgent in the old man's pale eyes. "Okay. We'll try it."

"He gets a remittance," said Lonely. "Not much, but enough for fodder. You won't have to pay him."

"He'll get paid what he earns," said Johnny.

Lonely shook his head. "Way I figure, either he won't earn a penny or it'll be so much you can't pay him."

"I follow," nodded Johnny. He carried his coat over his arm, going to the door. "It's a deal."

"You might regret it. On the other hand, you might not. According to where you finally stand."

"I stand on my two feet."

"So you say." Lonely opened the door, waited for Johnny to go through, then followed. Amsy Buchanan had gone and Jarret was waiting, razor in hand, all smiles. Two of Field's hands, Shade and Halliday, were knocking the pool balls around in the other room. They jerked their heads at Johnny but did not speak to Lonely. The prospector, ignoring them, went out through the street door.

Johnny climbed into the chair and leaned back. Jarret came beaming, said, "Better cut that mop, hadn't I?"

"Plum forgot." He sat upright again. Neither of the Field riders could shoot pool to keep himself warm, Johnny thought. The shears caught a shaft of light as they snickered around his head. He felt drowsy. Jarret never stopped talking but he only heard parts of it.

". . . and Morg made the town. He cleaned it and pressed it like a suit of clothes . . . Morg is responsible for everything good we got . . . Morg is a man to tie to, until hell freezes over . . . Never forget it, Morg's the man around here . . . The Jenkins place can be made to pay if Morg's on your side and you ain't shiftless like Jenkins."

There was a loud and profane shout, then Shade and Halliday were arguing over a pool shot. Jarret droned on, but now he was completely drowned out. Johnny closed his eyes.

A pool ball slammed against the wall. Johnny came

awake with a start. Jarret's shears had nicked his left ear, there was blood on the towel.

"Hold still, Mr. Bracket, I'll fix it," said Jarret. His hands were shaking. He did not so much as glance at the room containing the pool table, where a two man riot was taking place. Arnie Frey, the cross-eyed man, came in the back door and joined in the turmoil.

There was no use talking to Jarret, that was plain. Johnny dabbed the towel at his ear, walking to the doorway of the pool room.

He said sharply, "All right, knock it down."

The three turned as one. They were, he realized, a working unit. They did not wear their guns which made them seem half-naked.

He went on, "I've been cut once. Just stop makin' the barber nervish, will you?"

Shade was the leader. He took one step forward to cement his position and said, "Now look, Bracket, you got no call to come over us just because Morg made a deal with you."

"Leave Morg out of it," Johnny suggested. "You've got the barber upset. So cut it out."

Shade took another step. "You ain't even said please, have you, Texas?"

When Halliday, who had been in such violent disagreement with the spokesman, spread out a step and Arnie Frey followed suit to form a wedge, Johnny knew that he was in a frame. He had the big barber's towel wadded in his left hand. He could hear Jarret whimper something behind him. They had set him up and he surmised it was either designed to test him or jealousy and fear regarding Morg Field.

He let Shade take another step. Then he went forward and said, "Why, I'd be glad to say please. Please get the hell out of here."

He hit Shade with the towel, so that it opened around his face, blinding him. Then he shot past the Field foreman and gained the pool table. Then he picked up the cue ball and threw it. The heavy round marble struck Shade in the small of the back and drove him forward, coughing. The six ball was next and Johnny banked it off the charging Halliday, so that it partially interfered with Arnie Frey. Then he saw Frey had a knife.

A pool cue came handy to his grasp. He swung it in a

short arc, reversed it and used it as a spear. The butt took care of Arnie, the tip seemed to go halfway through the middle of Halliday, who screamed like a wounded eagle.

Shade was still coughing. Johnny went past him to the chair, retaining his hold on the pool stick. He sat down and said, "Better start a new towel."

Jarret stammered, "I can't. . . . I'm shakin' like a leaf."

Johnny said, "Why, so you are. Gimme the razor."

He stirred lather in a thick mug, watching the Field riders. They were slow in recovering. Pool hall equipment made a splendid armory, Johnny thought. He remembered his brother Toole cleaning out a barroom one night with the sixteen balls and the butt of a cue.

He applied the lather, began to shave. He could see the pool room in the mirror. Shade was up first, the others staggered against the table, holding various parts of their anatomy.

He called to them, "Shame on you, a Sunday morning and you actin' like that. Don't you know any better?"

The language they used was also unbefitting the Sabbath. He turned to look at them, razor held suggestively in his fist. "You, with the knife, I might have hurt you bad. Now just run along and when you try again—better bring your guns."

The last phrase snapped at them. They responded with jerks of their heads, staring at him through pain, hating him.

Shade coughed, "When we do, it'll be curtains, you lowdown, lily-livered hound pup."

"It'll be curtains," nodded Johnny. "Maybe all around. We'll see about that, won't we, boys? And until then, a civil tongue in the head."

Shade opened his mouth, but the cross-eyed Frey nudged him. He stopped, swallowing hard. The three of them made their way out onto the street. They were hobbling on their high heels. They headed for The Four Aces and Johnny watched them out of sight before he resumed shaving.

Jarret said in a low voice, "Only mistake Morg made, bringing them in. He don't need guns. Why does he have to keep them around?"

"You been singin' a song about him like he's an angel," said Johnny. "How come you don't know that answer?"

"Tom Mulloy keeps the law. We don't need men like them."

Johnny wiped the lather from his face. He didn't look too

bad, he thought, peering into the mirror. He wasn't handsome like Toole, nor dashing like Sam. He resembled Joe more than the brothers, who took after his mother's side. Maybe that's why he and Joe fought all the time.

He said, "How much do I owe you for the damage?"

"Nothing," said Jarret. "I owe you, for saving the place. They'd have busted it up."

Johnny put a silver dollar on the shelf where the razor and mug were kept. "Forget it. I appreciate the bath more than a dollar's worth. Thanks."

"Thank *you*, Mr. Bracket," said the barber. "I know Morg'll be glad you whupped those boys. Although how you did it, I don't know."

"You want to know something?" Johnny set his hat to one side of his head. "I'll get along whether Morg backs me up or not. Keep the peace, friend."

He went out on Main Street. People were walking sedately toward the church. He sauntered, enjoying the clear air, looking for Field or Lonely or maybe the girl, although he had an idea Miss Carter would not be welcomed at the services. He walked along like any citizen, thinking that this was a nice town, that he would be happy to settle here, that he had not seen a place in Texas or anywhere else that he liked the look of so well.

He almost bumped into Lonely. There was a young woman with the prospector. Johnny tore off his hat.

"Johnny Bracket," said Lonely. "This here's my granddaughter, Mary Jones."

She had copper hair under a small, neat bonnet. Her eyes were narrow and slanting and had in them the sort of color and depth that promised without inviting. She was wrapped against the weather in a long cloak. Her shoulders were high and she was trim and slim. Her mouth was rather wide and the lower lip was full and rich.

"I'm real proud to meet you, Miss Jones." He found that he could look straight into her eyes, she did not turn away.

"Mr. Bracket. I understand you're settling here."

"Seems that way."

Lonely said, "Always walk her to the church door. Never go in, the shebang might fall down and kill all the good folks in there."

"I'll be more than happy to oblige," said Johnny. "Me,

I don't worry about the other folks. I got plenty to worry about . . . namely, me."

Lonely seemed to evaporate and he was walking with the girl. She was about twenty-two, he thought, long past marriageable age in this country, but she was as fresh and dewy as a yellow Texas rose. He thought of the sultry girl he had met last night, imagined the two of them together, shook his head at the comparison.

She said, "You don't like being shanghaied into walking a lady to church, do you?"

"I purely love it," he said hastily. "I was thinkin' of somethin' altogether different."

"Yes?" She waited for the answer.

He said with all the Bracket smoothness, "I was thinkin' how lucky I got, all of a sudden. Had a dream about my Papa last night. He was all wrong. I got to meet you, all for nothin'."

"At no cost, you mean?"

"Just for free. And it's a wonderful feeling," he told her.

She smiled generously, but her eyes did not change. She was looking beyond him and he saw Morg Field coming from behind The Four Aces. It occurred to him that this might be slightly embarrassing, since everyone must know about the woman upstairs. He was astounded when Morg fell in step on the other side of Mary Jones.

She said, "Good morning, Morg." And she smiled, as one does to an old friend on a fine winter Sunday morning.

"Mary, my dear." He took her elbow, looking at Johnny. "I see you met our newest neighbor."

"Yes, indeed. Grandfather, you know."

Morg laughed heartily, "Yes, I know."

They both seemed highly amused but Johnny did not savor the implication. He said, "Excuse me, I see a man I have to talk with."

He took off his hat, bowed to them, hurried down an alley between two frame houses. He caught Monty Carruthers just as the Britisher lowered a small bottle from his lips.

"Er—bad show, eh?" Carruthers corked the flask and put it in his pocket. "Sort of thought I might quit, you know. Seems like I'm not for it today."

Johnny said thoughtfully, "Does it have anything to do with Mary Jones and Morg Field?"

Monty looked long and carefully at him. Then he said, "Perhaps Lonely is right, at that."

"People and events move quick in Field City," Johnny said. "I think I changed my mind about church. I think we better ride out to the Jenkins place."

"I'm not at all certain about it," said Monty. "It is a fact that I shall finish this bottle before noon."

"We can go into that later. A boozer with your experience shouldn't get drunk on a lousy half pint," said Johnny. "And anyway, it's good manners to offer a touch to a friend, where I come from."

Carruthers reluctantly brought forth the bottle. Johnny tipped it, watching his companion from the corner of an eye. When Monty winced, he took a breath and handed back the diminished whiskey.

"We could hire a buggy," he said. "Unless you'd rather ride one of my ponies."

"By all means a carriage." Carruthers hesitated. "Morg's not going to approve, you know."

"What's he got against you?"

"Several things. Do you mind?"

"I keep tellin' people," Johnny complained. "Do I have to tell everyone in town that I'm on my own?"

"Probably. But when will you be forced to tell it to Morgan Field?"

There seemed no reason to answer, so Johnny led the way to the livery stable.

# chapter four

THE HORSE WAS a hammerhead buckskin and it could pull. The buggy wheels squeaked in frozen ruts, protested as Johnny swung up a narrow, steep road toward the Jenkins place which was on a level plateau. Monty finished the whiskey and tossed the bottle into a clump of dead brush.

Johnny said, "The creek is over yonder, I see." He could hear the stream running hard beneath ice floes. "That's good water."

"Comes down from Morg Field's high country," said Monty. "He could dam it up any time, you see."

"He could if his men could hold the dam."

"Oh, but they can."

The buckskin toiled upwards, made a right turn and they could see the Jenkins place. Johnny reined in, looking back down the slope, then at the stream, then at the buildings a hundred yards ahead. "This place could be held, too, if it so happened."

Monty said, "So could Jericho, they thought."

They drove on. The house ahead was built of strong and heavy logs. The barn was inadequate, Johnny thought at once, and the corral bars lay helter skelter. There was something wrong with the entire picture, each detail was awry. The roof had holes in it which did not seem weather-battered. The windows were black apertures, staring empty-eyed, more tragic than forlorn.

Monty muttered, "It's foreboding."

"How long has it been empty?"

"Since the fall round-up."

"Why, that's only a few months."

"Yes. Looks like years of desolation, eh? Reason enough, as you shall see."

There was a well in the yard. Johnny looked in; it seemed clean enough. They blanketed the horse, anchored him with an iron weight and walked slowly around the house.

Monty said, "The barn needs shoring up, you see. Not a task for two men, we'll need help. However, not a great job, either. Shall we go in through the kitchen?"

Johnny followed the little Britisher, feeling more and more the brooding quality of the place. When he saw the door hanging crooked on its hinges he stopped and examined it with care. He fingered round holes in the battens.

"Rifle bullets," he said.

"What did you expect? Jenkins was a shiftless man with a certain arrogance. He was a brave one, also."

"They chased him out?"

"They buried him on Boot Hill, just east of town."

"I see," said Johnny. He went into the kitchen. There was a dry sink and a stove with its pipes down and a rickety chair. Snow had frozen beneath a gap in the roof. Rusting pots hung on the wall. The table was a slab with its surface skinned by ricocheting lead. "Looks like they had quite a war."

There was a room which contained a mouldering bed, a splintered chest of drawers and a clothes cabinet against the wall, bullet holes everywhere. He yanked out a drawer and a small book fell to the floor.

He looked at the accounts of the late Jenkins with an interested eye. Water had made it somewhat illegible but a last entry was plain to be read, "Paid Morg Field in full, $2,000, damn his soul to hell."

Monty looked at it and said, "Jenkins borrowed from the bank, of course. His sin lay in declaring himself independent. I must add, he was careless with his running irons. He had two hired men from Montana, real toughs, who ran when the big fight occurred."

The house was suddenly oppressive. They went out back. A sheer cliff rose from behind the barn, protecting the buildings from the north side. It lent a coziness to the property, gave sense to it, made it somewhat cleansed of the stultification Johnny had felt.

There was pasturage in a sheltered valley bounding the creek. Beyond was high grass, a mesa flattened out in the near distance. A man could begin here and work and, all else equal, he could prosper. Northward and westward the mountain range lay pure and snowcapped against the Sunday sky.

"You had to learn how things were," said Monty. "You see, old man Lonely took a fancy to you."

"Lonely, I take it, is quite an hombre."

"Yes. His son founded the town, you know. Called it Hope City. Ironic, isn't it?"

"Hope City? What kind of fella was he?"

"A dreamer. He came here when his wife died in Denver. Lonely was prospecting in the desert. After Harry died, leaving Mary alone, he came here and took over what was left."

"Morg Field again?"

"It wasn't necessary for Field to do anything. Harry was quite impractical. The frontier wasn't ready for him."

"Well, then, Morg just took over. That it?"

"Lonely says any man without conscience and with enough courage can take over a dying town. The mining petered out. Morg brought cattle. Morg was the savior."

Johnny walked to the barn, looked in at the ravaged bunkhouse. He returned to the yard and stood looking down toward the creek.

Monty said, "Forewarned is forearmed. Jenkins was a fool."

"Field's men killed him?"

"Unknown persons, attacking in the night. Mulloy was never able to find proof and the sheriff wisely remains clear of Field City. Elections are nominal, of course."

"When's the next election?"

"In springtime, May 15th."

"I'd be wise not to take Field's offer, you think?"

"Who knows what course a man should take? In town there are Amsy Buchanan and a Mexican named Pedro Armindez, perhaps some who dare not allow themselves to be known as opposing the powers that be. There is also Lonely Jones."

"And you?"

"A drunken exile." The pink cheeks became dark red. "Do not count on me, except to try to rebuild here, if you so decide."

"Tell me about Morg Field and Mary Jones."

Monty looked away, moved restlessly. "She has a bit of her father in her. She likes to believe there is good in everyone. It is a fine trait, you know."

Johnny pondered for a moment. Then he said, "Well, here's the way it is. Beggars can't be choosers. Maybe Mary Jones is right, we'll never know if we don't give it a riffle. If you're game to help me put it back together, I'm game to try to make it stick."

He offered his hand. Monty took it diffidently, but his round face seemed a bit thinner, his shoulders straightened, his eyes brightened.

"Done and done," he said.

They returned to the carriage. Johnny uncovered the buck-skin and turned his head for home, letting him choose his own pace, sunk in deep thought. Monty was equally silent as the miles went slowly underfoot.

Now that Johnny was considering settling on the ranch, attempting to work it, he remembered the first place, the one from which he had run away and had been brought back in disgrace. That was in Grayson County, Texas, in the Red River region, where Joe, his father, had put down his first founda-tion and tried, but failed, to raise his family under a com-munal roof.

Joe was a violent man from the cradle; that was a known

fact. Comanches had learned of him in Grayson County and the neighbors and the preacher, who was an ass, but mostly his sons had learned it. In those days nothing was funny, everything was deadly serious because of the ranch. It was dull and not to be stood by a boy like Johnny, and in truth Sam and Toole did not take to it very well. They were all gone before Joe ever got done half what he had planned.

Later, when they had moved to the bigger place near Fort Worth and Ma had died and Pa remarried, Johnny had escaped for good. His two brothers had already departed, and Joe was not so violent but not a peaceable man, either.

Only now, in prospect of taking over the Jenkins place, things looked a bit different. A man trying to ranch it needed all the waking hours of work he could get. Sleep was only to be for regaining strength. Three sons should have been enough to make the Bracket ranches pay. Joe had himself a point there.

Joe was making it fine, now, on the third ranch, near El Paso, and it occurred to Johnny that he had sold out and moved to West Texas only after his sons had settled that far the other side of the mountains. He was always grumping and buffaloing and hallooing and raising Ned, but he brought the good looking wife away from her folks to a place where he could be in the same general geography that his sons frequented, always complaining that none would settle down, always bawling at them when they came near, but staying on the ranch, making it pay and, without ever saying so, making it a headquarters for them. Not that they often used it, but it was a comfort, away up here in the Territory, to know that Sam, Toole and Joe could always be reached through the home ranch.

Now, also, he would be putting to use all the things he had assimilated through being raised on a ranch. Joe had never failed, he could always make a place pay. There were certain solid, basic duties to attend, each and every day according to the season, there was the knowledge of cattle, and many whys and wherefores which Johnny could not have recited on notice, but which he knew as well as he knew his name. Joe had hammered a good bit into him with iron hands.

He drove into Field City alongside the silent Englishman and put the horse up at Amsy Buchanan's and headed for

The Four Aces Saloon. It was late afternoon, now. Outside
the door, Monty stopped.

"I'll just go by Lonely's and speak a bit with him."

"No drink?"

"Odd, you know. Looking at the place out there, thinking
of all that must be done, my thirst has quite vanished." He
added quickly, "For tonight. No promises."

"Sure, no promises," said Johnny. "I'll pick you up tomorrow after my business with Field is done. Have a list ready,
huh?"

"Pedro will provide help," said Monty. "Good men. They
do not often see hard cash. Agreed?"

"Hasta luego," said Johnny. He went into the saloon.
Susan Carter was seated at the table in the corner. Simon
Jarret was at the bar, talking away at the greasy-haired
barkeeper. Four citizens looked up from a desultory game
of pan, then looked away quickly, as though intent on minding their own business.

Johnny went directly to the girl, sat down. She glanced
at him without smiling, but continued to look.

"Good evenin', Miss Carter," he said. "Buy you a glass
of wine?"

"Nobody buys wine for me," she said. "Please have your
whiskey."

Johnny raised a hand. The bartender came promptly, expressionless. "Wine for the lady and whiskey for me. The
good whiskey."

In a moment the drinks were in front of them. The dark
girl sighed, lifted a lovely shoulder.

"Texans," she said. "Always for trouble."

"Me? Why, I was born in Mississippi," said Johnny. "Pa
brought us West when I was a yearling."

"Texans are never born, they are made," she said.

"Could be. You expectin' Morg Field?"

"Expecting? That's not quite the word. He'll be here."

"Then I'll wait."

"He'll be here in ten minutes. He has left the Jones house
and gone to the cantina."

"I guess everybody knows every move every other body
makes in this town," said Johnny. "One reason I never
cottoned to towns."

"When Morg Field moves, everyone notices."

"And reports to you."

"No."

"Oh." He detected the undertone of jealousy, of frustration. He saw her eyes go Indian bright, then dull as she raised the wine glass. He went on quickly, "I'm about to make a deal with him."

"I know."

"You got anything to tell me?" he asked boldly, looking into the black eyes.

For a moment he thought she was angry, then she said in little more than a whisper, snarling, "Just watch your pants, sonny, he might steal 'em."

He laughed, startled. "I reckoned that."

"You can't reckon it deep enough." Her gaze shifted beyond him, over his shoulder, and he saw that Morg Field had come in silent as the night. Now, as Johnny turned in his chair, the three riders, Shade, Halliday and Frey filed and stood behind Field. Johnny slung his coat open to show he was unarmed and got up from the chair, balancing on his wide-spread feet.

Field said, "No, Johnny. Listen to me." He gestured. Shade led the three men forward. First they spoke to Jarret, flat against the bar, pallid with fear.

"We're sorry, Simon, real sorry. We'll pay for the damage." They moved and faced Johnny, and Shade said, "Reckon Saturday's booze roiled up Sunday mornin'. We didn't mean nothin'."

"Okay, forget it," said Johnny.

"Well . . . that's the way it is." Shade shuffled awkwardly, then turned and led the others out of the saloon.

Field came to the table and sat down, tossing a heavy bearskin coat to the bartender. "Heard you went out to the Jenkins place. What do you think?"

"It can work."

"It can be made into a fine ranch."

"It can be," said Johnny. "Soon as we plug up the bullet holes, we'll move out there."

"You said 'we', meanin' the Britisher?"

"He hired out to mend the fences."

"He's a no-good drunk."

"Your friend, Lonely Jones, didn't mince words about that. Said Monty wanted a chance."

"Givin' a chance to a fool is a waste. I can get you all the help you need."

Johnny said cheerfully, "Now, you wouldn't want to hire my men for me, would you, Morg? I mean, I'm borrowin' money from your bank, and all that, but it ain't personal, is it?"

"What do you mean, personal?"

"Bank's a public institution, my Pa always said. You got the ranch and everything I own as collateral. If it ain't worth the deal, why make it?"

"You know it ain't worth it," said Field. "I'm loaning mainly on your head."

Johnny leaned toward the big man and asked softly, "And Jenkins? What kind of deal did he make?"

Field leaned back, averting his face. "Jenkins was a man to make enemies."

"But he paid you off before he made one too many."

"Yes. He paid off."

"You figure he swung a wide loop to get the money?"

"I figure he sold me some of my own cattle."

"And you and those men of yours couldn't outsmart him on that?"

Morg Field said sullenly, "Jenkins was smart enough. He was lazy, shiftless, but smart."

"Too smart?"

"Whoever killed him must've thought so."

"Whoever killed him got to the top of that hill either in the night, or because he knew 'em and let 'em get up there," said Johnny. "Either way it don't figure. Not for a smart man. It could be he was killed by enemies he figured was friends."

"Cattle thieves don't know friendship."

"I see. You reckon he was dealin' with rustlers and they crossed him."

"He probably crossed them and got paid off."

"All right," said Johnny. "Now, I ain't a thief. I want that understood. I aim to buy a bull and breed my stuff. I also aim to hire who I want and them I hire will see to it nobody else gets ideas about swingin' a wide loop. And I intend mindin' my own business and that people leave me alone and do the same. That suit you, Morg?"

"Why, that's all it takes to get along here." The good humor was restored, the smile flashed wide and warm.

"Then we won't hear no more about Monty Carruthers nor anybody else I want to work for me."

"Certainly not. I was only warnin' you."

"That's fine," said Johnny mildly. "I appreciate it."

"Tomorrow morning at ten, I'll be in the bank with everything made out for you to take over."

"Just dandy," said Johnny. He finished his whiskey. "See you in the mornin', then." He bowed deeply to the dark girl, who nodded once, then resumed her wine glass. He got his sheepskin-lined coat and went to the hotel.

At the desk he asked for paper, pencil and envelope. He went upstairs, took off his hat and coat, cleared the stand which held the water pitcher and basin, sat down on the straight chair and began laboriously to compose a letter to his father.

"Pa, I'm up here in the Territory and I just made a deal with a man named Morg Field who was down around El Paso some years back, afore you got there I reckon. You might could look him up as I figger he is a no-good bastard. But up here he has got the town hog-tied and I am getting a toe-holt on a ranch which ain't such a bad proposition if I hang loose and last awhile. I got the stockers through, a few of them anyways and this galoot is puttin up some money which he figgers I will blow back to him. He figgers I will not make it and he will have the place or I will make it and he can blast me off or maybe even I do make it and join him and we become pardners, only this galoot will sure swallow any pardners might they think they are in a good deal with him . . ."

It was amazing how much he could put down. He had to go and get more paper from the desk man and it was dark before he finished and his hand ached something terrible.

It was an especially odd thing that he should write such a letter since this was the first one he had ever sent to his father.

# chapter five

PEDRO ARMINDEZ was a thin man with a long upper lip like a mule and a knife scar drawn diagonally from his left eye downward to his jawbone. He spoke excellent English when addressing Monty or other trusted friends.

He said, "I will send Manuelito and Diego. They can saw and hammer. I will send Jose because he is strong as bull, he can haul and pull."

Monty said, "Thank you and God bless you."

"It is this, we must never cease to try," said Pedro. "If we continue, perhaps some day, our children will be free."

Johnny said, "Better for your people here than it is where I come from."

"But not good enough," said Pedro Armindez, his head high and proud. "Not while such men as Rag Shade can kick us from his path while Morgan Field looks the other way."

"What about elections? You're all citizens."

"Without votes," said Pedro. "That is what we work and try for. The right to exercise our rights."

Monty explained, "They keep the Mexican-Americans away by threats. Pedro votes, and a few others. But mainly they are afraid."

"I see." It was an expression he had used rather too often to suit him, because he didn't really 'see' at all. He merely learned more and more about how Morg Field ran the town. He told himself it was none of his business, but found that he could not refrain from glancing curiously at Pedro and his lovely young wife, Consuela, as he drank tequila in the low-ceilinged cantina which they owned and operated. They were fine looking people, from head to toe. They had offered help without reservation when Lonely and Monty had approached them.

He said, "Time makes changes. I got to say it will take me some good time to get established. A year, maybe two, three years."

"We can wait," said Pedro.

"Even then, I can't promise nothin'," said Johnny lamely. "I don't even know all that goes on."

"No one *knows*, except Morgan Field. We surmise," said Monty Carruthers. "All we can do is go along with a new man, such as yourself, hoping he will be strong enough to match Field."

"I ain't even sure I want to do anything about Field. This is the nicest little town I was ever in," said Johnny. "He built it, everyone says."

"No, Señor. Harry Jones, he built it. Morgan Field, he stole it," said Pedro.

It might be true, thought Johnny, wearily. It had been a hard day, hiring a wagon and draught horses to pull it, buying supplies and tools and timber and shingles and stoves and whatnot until his head ached with figures and spending the newly borrowed money.

He again thanked Armindez and went to the wagon. He drove to the bank, where he turned in vouchers signed by him to a young man named Randolph Holt, who was pale and thin and round-shouldered, but had a nice, easy smile and large, honest blue eyes.

"I'll take care of it, Mr. Bracket," he said. "It's nice knowing the Jenkins place is going to be used again. It's good property, believe me."

"You know the place?"

"My father had it before Jenkins," Holt said. "When he died, Mom sold it and sent me to school with the money. She didn't want me to work on a ranch."

"Uh-huh. You got a pretty good job here?" He looked at the young man's slim, white hands and the narrow shoulders.

Holt flushed. "It's all right."

"I see." There went that meaningless expression again. He saw, all right, that this nice, weak boy wouldn't get to base one with Morg Field. It took a bully boy with a lot of brass to make it with the banker. Mom Holt had just as well saved her money. "Well, come see us when you can."

He was to meet Monty at the Jones place. He found it on a side street without difficulty, a white frame house built close to the ground. He knocked and Mary Jones opened the door, smiling at him.

"You're just in time for tea."

"That'll be fine, with a little whiskey in it," he said. "Howdy, Mr. Jones."

Lonely was lowered into a deep-seated chair, seeming somehow out of place indoors, relaxed, spectacles on the tip of his nose, a periodical in his hand.

"Set and Mary'll bring you the whiskey," said Lonely. Like many silent men, he could and would talk at home, among family and friends. "Hear you had a little trouble yesterday mornin'."

"It wasn't trouble, it was a pleasure," said Johnny. He was watching Mary move across the room in a grey, clinging dress of some soft material. She wasn't as slim as he had thought. It was the way she carried herself, head high, shoulders back that gave her the proud look. Her wide mouth was tucked upwards, her lips moist and parted as she poured the liquor into hot tea at his elbow.

Dark girl, fair girl, he thought, who would think Field City could hold two so different, each beautiful? He said, however, anticipating Lonely, "Morg had them come in like little men and apologize. It didn't seem right to me."

"If you mean they ain't the apologizin' kind, you're wrong. Morg broke 'em. He found out you can cover up a lot of mischief by sayin' you're sorry, you didn't really mean it."

"Still, those three are gunfighters. Men like that, they're mean clear through."

"Yep. Mean as poison. But Morg broke 'em. Gives you an idea."

"He's a powerful man, all right," said Johnny. "I note Miss Mary is friendly to him."

"Oh, he's been courtin' her for a couple years. Gettin' ready to run for Mayor now we got the town all corporated and such. Morg feels he needs respectability."

The girl sat down, her knees together, the smile unchanged. "He's responsible for every advance the town has made. So long as he has its interest at heart he isn't completely bad."

"Mary thinks of the town like it's part hers," Lonely explained. "A heritage. Howsomever, Jarret tells a fancy story 'bout you yesterday mornin'. He bein' a Morg Field man, it sounded good."

Johnny said with care, "I've got to say, I'm not against Morg. I'm not for him, either. I borrowed from his bank, like I told him. We get along."

"You see?" Mary addressed her father. "You have to take the bitter with the better."

"I don't have to take anything," said the prospector. "I just wait until the weather breaks, then hit the trail. The mountains will look good this springtime." He got up and stretched, a marvelously supple man, although he must have been sixty, Johnny thought. "Meantime, I got things to do out back. We'll be out to see you when you get the place decent, Johnny."

He walked out of the room and Mary squinted at Johnny, winking one eye. "He's giving us our heads."

For a moment Johnny didn't answer. His usual glibness would be out of place at this moment. There was something in that wink, some urchin quality, some deep warmth that made him wish suddenly and totally that he could share all his secrets with Mary Jones.

His voice was unusually deep and serious when he spoke. "There's got to be some kind of start to everything."

She lifted her teacup, put it down without tasting the hot liquid. Her eyes deepened, changed color. "I won't say I don't know what you mean."

"Why should I be sore and upset when Morg came along yesterday mornin' the way he did?" he asked both the girl and himself. "I'd just said howdy to you."

"Why should I be disappointed when you went away so quick?"

"Your grandfather's a medicine man."

"A he-witch," she suggested, still surveying him, as though examining him, what kind of man he was, where he came from, where he was going, everything about him.

His own mind teemed with thoughts, increasing desires, wonder, admiration of her directness. He had experienced much with women but none as honest and forthright. He said, "The funny part is, you mean it."

"Oh, yes. My father was that kind of man. He taught me to show myself, not to be afraid. The moment we met there was something."

"Something. I wonder . . ." The sound at the door broke the spell.

Both turned frowning, as though brought back from some far, pleasant place. Then she made a gesture of regret and apology and went to the door.

Morg Field stood there. He was holding upright the small, dilapidated figure of Monty Carruthers. The Englishman was hopelessly, pitifully drunk.

Field said gravely, "He said he was to meet you here, Johnny."

"That's right." Johnny surveyed the pair. "Where'd you find him?"

"In back of the saloon. He bought a bottle from the Mexicans. Used your money, of course."

"Why not? He works for me."

"Why not? Well, maybe because he's a lousy investment," said Field. "Look at him."

Lonely Jones appeared, moving softly across the room. He said, "I'll take care of him."

"No," said Johnny. "My job."

"You can't go out there with only him, like this," said Field. "What good will it do?"

"More good than leavin' him in town," said Johnny. He was cheerful enough. "Just gimme a hand with him, huh? There's a buffalo robe under the seat."

Morg Field lifted the semi-conscious figure without aid, carried him to the wagon and found space as Johnny produced the robe. The two stood together for a moment, their breath mingling on the evening air, white and frosty. Monty looked like a disreputable cherub with only his nose sticking out from the wrapping.

Field said, "You're a damfool Texan. I want you to make good out there. This is a bad start."

Johnny said, "You make your starts, I'll make mine. Okay, Morg?"

Then he turned and walked quickly back to the house and pointedly closed the door behind him before Field could fashion a reply. He went to Mary, who held his coat in her hands. Lonely stood in the doorway, his head cocked to one side, his faded eyes intent.

"I heard somethin' once," Johnny said. "Spoken by an Englishman, it was. It went like this: 'Nothin' disposes a man toward understanding like knowin' he's understood.' Reckon we'll try it on for size, thataway."

Lonely said, "Just a try, Johnny. If Monty can't make it, at least we've tried."

Mary went with him to the door. She said, "We'll meet again soon."

"Oh, yes. Work is to do, then we meet, soon." He touched her arm and the skin was warm and alive and he thought it was like no other flesh he had ever known. He went quickly to the wagon, made sure Monty had not come unraveled and pulled a horse blanket about his own knees. He waved to her. There was no sight of Morg Field.

He drove out toward the ranch. JB Ranch, it would be now, with his brand on each head of cattle, his own house and barn and corral and henhouse and bunkhouse and trees and grass . . . He broke off. His own, with a mortgage.

The sun was going down behind the last hill and the wind was coming up. He yanked his hat low over his brow. He would be chilled on the outside when he got to the place, but inside he was warm enough.

A brave speech he had made, about understanding. He knew where he had heard it, from Toole, his brother. Now that he was founding a home his thoughts turned oftener to his family. Toole was the bright one, went to school, read books and magazines and newspapers, wound up working for Wells Fargo. He was the rash one, too, the one who always preferred to take chances.

Had he, Johnny, understood Toole? Or Sam, the steady-going Marshal of cowtowns?

Or Joe, his father?

Easy to talk. Easy, maybe, to understand a woman like Mary Jones, because that was something else again, a beginning, a new thing promising pleasure. Understanding his family, that was different.

Being the youngest hadn't made it easy, of course. They had put him in the soup too often, among them. They had made a goat and a beast of burden of the kid, and their ridicule had been hard to take.

On the other hand, he thought with new insight, all he knew he had learned from them. The way to do things right, the stubborn will to work he had from them. Nothing was impossible, they always said. If another man can do it, why can't we? And they had done, mostly, what they willed.

He drove, remembering them, listening to the call of the coyote in the hills, that night-song. He was hungry after awhile, but he could not push the horses. It was uphill most of the way. He resolutely put his mind on plans, how he would sleep tonight in the bunkhouse, eating cold food, drinking his own well water. Monty would be a problem, he thought, he might have to make a fire to get something into Monty. Well, that was all right, too.

In the morning they would work. He could not bring his cattle and cow ponies out until there was a place for them, until he knew the lay of the land and where and what to do about them. Amsy Buchanan was willing to care for them, at a small fee. That was all right, too.

In the morning Monty would work—or he would cut stake and move on. There was only one way with the boozers, knock it out of them with the club of hard work, so that they would not have time for the drink. There had been a time, right after Mom died, when Pa was going that way, but he had cured himself with labor from early bright to late dark.

The weather was clear and the wagon wheels made the lonely, whistling sound of metal tire on frozen ground and his nose and cheeks were cold. He swung one arm to restore circulation.

Well, then, he thought, I am in a new country, unlike Texas as can be, among people who are good, bad and indifferent. I have a place to go to work with. I have got what Pa said I should have; and it is up to me to make it work.

And I have killed a man. He looked up at the stars and said aloud, "Lord, I had to kill him to stay alive my own self. I didn't want to, I never wanted to kill a man. Forgive me, Lord."

He had no idea whether Anyone heard him. There were stars twinkling, and cloud formations marched across a yellow, winter moon. If there was Anything or Anyone, maybe he had squared himself. If there was Anyone or Anything, the one thing He or It must have is understanding.

## chapter six

ON ELECTION DAY in mid-May, Monty stood and looked back at the buildings and said, "Did it, all right. Amazing in a way. And I'm still sober."

There was paint on the house, the barn glowed red in the sun. The corral fence was straight as a ruler, Johnny thought with pride. When Monty did anything, it was shipshape, that was for sure.

In the north pasture the cattle grazed on early grass. There was a Hereford bull, now, a brawny beast with fiery eyes, dehorned but ready to butt himself into hell. The money was about gone, but they could live off the garden and the hens and the pigs and an occasional beef. They made their own bread and today they would take the buckboard into the celebration and bring back kitchen supplies such as salt, flour, molasses, sugar, coffee, canned tomatoes and peaches.

"You did good, Monty," he said fondly. "You did better

than good. If you wanta bust loose this trip, you got more'n a right."

The Britisher was tanned with winter and spring sun, he had grown a light-colored moustache clear across his broad upper lip, he walked with strength and pride. "Shouldn't be bothered, you know. Cost of gettin' over it is far too high."

"You haven't had a drink since New Year's."

"Don't require one," said Monty. He was wearing his city clothing, tight-fitting brown suit, low-heeled boots, high-crowned stiff hat. His shirt was white and immaculate, adorned by a high stock. "My patrimony will be spent for higher items in the scale."

"Like a poker game?"

"Quite possibly."

Johnny grinned. He had spent the long, solitary winter nights wearing out several decks of cards with Monty. There had been some progress, he thought, but not enough. "You'll never make it. You just ain't a poker player, pardner."

"Peculiar thing," said Monty, "nothin' I want to do more, you know, than to become expert at the game."

They climbed into the buckboard. The team leaned into the creak of oiled leather, soft and sibilant, the road was all downhill and shady going to town in May.

The JB Ranch was the talk of the county. Monty's engineering had brought water to the house, to the garden. Johnny's innate neatness had been responsible for the paint. The women for miles around came to peer and to compliment them, then to go home and complain.

It had been the finest winter of Johnny's life thus far. He had seen Mary Jones at Thanksgiving, Christmas, New Year's and several times since. He had risked a good horse in bitter February and March weather to spend a Saturday evening at the little white house in Field City.

After the first enormous stride, the affair had simmered down, for obvious reasons. He had no right to propose until the mortgage was paid off, he thought. She seemed content to let things ride, too satisfied, perhaps, since she still saw and smiled upon Morg Field. Many an unhappy hour went by when Johnny thought of this circumstance, and yet he could, in all conscience, do nothing about it.

The winter had gone by uneventfully except for work progress. Now it was Morg Field's time to bloom, with late springtime. There was no question of the election. His opponent was that sterling master of shears and razor, Simon Jarret. Field City had got its incorporation papers, some new people had moved in when the weather broke, the sawmill was busy, the bank was making money.

The horses jogged along, traces slack, brake holding smoothly. Monty rode with the jounces, back bone straight. He had been the best of companions. He had been the hardest of workers, bossing the Mexican crew with gentle firmness, so that they went back to town with newfound determination to do their jobs with perfection.

The Mexican-Americans had set up their own construction company under the patronage of Armindez. Manuelito and Pedro had learned much from Monty. Jose dug the foundations, the others built the houses and their business had prospered. A flock of newcomers from New Mexico and Texas had come in with the first thaw.

Yes, thought Johnny, it had been a good winter. He let the team run the last mile across the flat and pulled in at Pedro Armindez's cantina. It was ten o'clock in the morning and the bar was closed, he remembered with regret, because the polls were open and the citizenry was voting for Morg Field . . .

Morg Field sat in the office of the bank, which was in the rear of the one-story brick building. Randolph Holt, ballot in hand, stood facing him, scraping and bowing a little, something for which he hated himself but which he could not for the life of him abandon. His mother called it his "good manners," and he had no way of telling her that it made him sick to display them.

Field said, "The Mexicans don't vote. You don't have to do anything about it, Holt, so don't turn pale. Just tell Mulloy we been countin' the votes and they're worse agin us than we thought. Get Rag and the boys and do some discouragin'."

"But won't people think . . ." Holt began.

"People in this town think what I want 'em to think," snapped Morg. His face was black with controlled rage. "There's plenty of those greasers came in too late to have a vote. Just make as though we can't tell 'em apart, or somethin'. And jump."

Randy Holt gulped but said, "All right, Mr. Field." He was the only white man in town who called Morg by the formal appellation. He went out into the bank. He put his ballot atop a high writing desk. He marked a vicious "X" opposite the name of Simon Jarret, folded the paper and ran out into the street.

Tom Mulloy was lounging in the entrance of the barber shop. Because Jarret was a candidate, however hapless, the voting was being conducted at the schoolhouse, which was down the street, across from the Protestant church. Randy Holt went close to him and delivered the message from Morg Field.

The Marshal grunted and said, "Okay, Randy. Run along, your Mom'll be lookin' for you to eat."

"Are you going to stop Armindez from voting?"

"Never you mind," said Mulloy. "Run on and stay out of it."

There was no use to protest. He went down to the schoolhouse. Mary smiled sweetly at him. He gulped, mute as usual in her presence, and cast his vote. He managed to stammer something and went outside and toward his home.

He worried constantly about everything, but mainly Mary Jones. He knew Morg Field would protect her from harm, but that was the worst part of it.

His mother was only forty-five, a pretty woman who fluttered through life, hands waving, voice birdlike. She caressed him and said, "Dinner's all ready. Ham and potatoes and gravy. Tuesday, you know. Or is it Wednesday? No . . . Tuesday, because of election. Did you vote for Morg?"

"Of course not," he said. She wouldn't believe him.

"Morg shouldn't require you to work on Election Day. No one else is working. I must talk to him again."

"No, Mom, please, not again. It does no good."

"It's time you should be paid more. Prices have gone up." She skipped into the kitchen and rattled dishes and pans. "We have to think of ourselves, no one else will. You're the handsomest and smartest boy in town. Morg has got to be reminded he's lucky to have you in the bank. Not that it isn't a privilege for us; it maintains our position, and that's important, but all the same we need more money. When you're cashier and a partner, then we'll show everyone, but meantime position doesn't buy groceries. We owe the store too much now."

She had said it all again, as she did every day. He sat at the table, head in hands for a moment, then jerked erect lest she catch him off guard. He spent his entire existence on guard against one thing or another.

Tom Mulloy went down the street toward the Mexican quarter, where Rag Shade was patrolling. He could see Halliday and Frey at opposite ends of the district.

Shade said, "All quiet. The wetbacks won't try to vote."

"Nemmine them. Keep the others away from the polls."

Shade's pale eyebrows shot up. "Armindez?"

"All of 'em."

Shade grinned. "It'll be a pleasure."

"No guns."

Shade raised his arms. He was not wearing a belt. "You know we ain't totin' iron."

"Better get a few more men."

"We got Moriarty and Swede and Cannon standin' by."

"Okay. I'll be around." He lounged back to Main Street. It wasn't a good idea, he thought, and it wasn't necessary, but Morg always knew what he was doing. At least, he had proven he was right since coming to the Territory. The training under Manny Freed had done Morg a lot of good.

Still, it wasn't enough. There was too much hard work involved in the ranching. Mulloy was a town man. The X-Y was a damned nuisance. It was hard to get anyone to stay out there and take care of the place. It was impossible to keep running back and forth and this spring he meant to do something about it.

Meantime, here was a nasty business if Armindez cared about voting. There were a few of them always voted. Sure, they were against Morg, they didn't have anything and Morg had everything. Opposition was something you always had to expect. There couldn't be enough votes for Simon Jarret to make the election even close.

Or could there be? He walked a few paces toward the bank, then stopped. No use talking to Morg, not now. There'd only be more confusion. Only thing to do was take orders. It had paid off this far.

Johnny Bracket sat in the patio behind the cantina and listened to the music of guitar and accordion. Pedro Armindez was supplying free tequila, Monty was gone to the livery stable with the buckboard and team, he knew Mary was busy at the polling booth, he was relaxed and happy.

Pedro said, "They won't let the newcomers vote." He spoke in Spanish, a different dialect than Johnny knew, but clearly. "It is illegal but they have no representation."

Manuelito said in broken English, "Those swetwacks. What they know? They don't compeesh."

"Nevertheless, it is against principle," said Pedro.

"Yes, it is," said Johnny, sucking a lemon, then drinking the tequila. "But does it matter?"

"We are different. We are from California," said Pedro. "Yet I believe they should have the vote."

"Nobody, least of all Jarret, is going to beat Morg Field," said Johnny. "You got to be practical. Now, if they stopped you from voting, that would be a horse from another stable."

A stripling with olive cheeks, out of breath, came in the rear door and whispered in Pedro's ear. The instruments ceased to play and some of the sunshine went out of the room.

Pedro stood up. He said to Johnny, "As you say. It is forbidden that anyone of Spanish blood shall vote today. A local ordinance, newly passed . . . by whom?"

Johnny said, "I wouldn't know by whom. Only, it don't go."

"Mulloy says it goes. Mulloy, his deputies and some others. Moriarty, Cannon, Swede."

Johnny said, "Never heard of 'em." He took another drink. "You want to vote?"

"I intend to vote."

"Meet you at the polls." He had taken a good bit of tequila, but his hands and feet were steady. He waved at big Jose, the diminutive Manuelito, the clever Diego. "Give me half an hour. Then be at the polls."

He was not conscious of indignation as he walked in the brisk May air toward the livery stable. He only felt light and free and determined. He had enjoyed working with the three Mexicans from California. They had done more than asked of them, more than he could afford to pay. Lonely Jones had been right about Monty, and the helpers had proven to be equally invaluable. It seemed nothing at all to make sure that they exercised their coveted right to vote in the local election.

Monty was not at the stable, nor was Amsy Buchanan. He rummaged in the buckboard and found his warbag. From it he took his gunbelt. He unwrapped the six-gun from its oilskin and wiped its polished surface. He loaded five chambers and slipped cartridges into the loops of the belt.

On second thought he went into Amsy's office and looked around. A shotgun was in the rack with a pair of rifles. He found shells and loaded the gun. He felt prepared when he went back on Main Street and walked toward the school-house.

He saw Mulloy, waved to him, continued on his way. The Marshal stared, then broke into a trot, following him.

"Hey. Johnny!"

He turned and waited. Mulloy came up, out of breath, eyes popping.

"Where you goin' with that arsenal?"

"Just takin' a walk," said Johnny. "I feel better with it on me."

"It's agin the law to carry arms on Election Day."

"Is it, now?" He looked pointedly at Mulloy's Colts.

"I am the law."

"Now, Tom, you know better'n that. No man is the law. You mean you represent the law."

"I represent Morg Field," said Mulloy. "That's law enough for me and you both."

Johnny shook his head. "You still got it wrong. Why, even local law can be cockeyed. Some crazy galoots have tried to say Pedro Armindez and his people can't vote. Now, Tom, you know that's impossible."

Mulloy scratched his jaw. "Law's law, Johnny. That's all there is to it. Now, put up them guns and go along and vote for Morg, like a good fella."

"Me? I don't live in town. I can't vote."

"Sure, you can. It's all right. Come on, we'll put the guns in my office."

He reached out a hand. Johnny stepped back a long yard.

"Tom, I'm not goin' to vote. I'm just seein' that other people get their rights under the Constitution."

"What Constitution? You loco, Johnny?"

"Nope. I ain't ignorant, either. I read the Constitution of the United States. All about the right to vote and the right to bear arms. Keep away, Tom."

He backed down the street, then turned and stalked to-ward the schoolhouse. Mulloy hesitated, fingered his gun butt, shook his head and wheeled toward the bank. At the street corner Johnny stopped and took out his railroad watch. The half hour had passed. He waited, leaning against the door of a building, watching both streets.

Armindez, Manuelito, Diego, Jose and three companions came from the house next to the cantina. They had, he saw, dressed themselves in fiesta costumes, broad scarlet sashes, slit trousers, boleros, wide sombreros with tasselled brims. They walked loosely, without rhythm, but with purpose as they came toward the corner.

He looked the other way, toward the schoolhouse. From The Four Aces Saloon came Shade, Frey, Halliday and three nondescript men of some swagger and muscle who must be the deputized Swede, Moriarty and Cannon. The street began to fill up behind them.

There were no women. Only men appeared, on the boardwalks, in the windows, in doorways. Amsy Buchanan lingered in front of the polling place, looking left and right. In a moment he was joined by Lonely Jones and Monty. They remained, indecisive, in the vicinity of the schoolhouse and Johnny knew they were thinking of Mary.

He stepped deeper into the doorway as Armindez and the others went by. They knew he was there but the deputies had not yet seen him. He thought about mobs he had seen. The airiness and lightness had left him.

Then he heard low, musical voices speaking a patois he understood and the street in the wake of Armindez and his men was littered with people. There were men, women and little children, chattering, curious. Their brown faces and deep liquid eyes went back and forth, he heard the word "liberty" in Spanish-Mexican. These were the newcomers from Texas and the Territories, people he knew all about, mercurial, brave, seeking always to better themselves, moving across the Border, then northward, seeking that ephemeral state they called freedom.

And he knew, standing there that in his light-hearted manner he might have inaugurated a riot.

He looked for Mulloy and Morg Field and did not see them. He looked at the tough deputies and saw Frey run back into the saloon as the first of the new Mexicans turned the corner, to emerge a moment later holding a sawed-down greener.

He saw Armindez put out his hand to stop his people when the weapon was shown. He saw the pouring of people from behind Armindez begin to press close, pushing the gaily clad local folk closer to Rag Shade and the bully boys behind him.

He heard Shade yell, "You dirty greasers, get back to your kennels."

He saw otherwise sane and sensible men dive into buildings for arms and ammunition. He saw Lonely start forward, to be restrained by Amsy and Monty. Now the others were arming themselves, so that only Shade, the leader, stood against the dark-skinned people without a weapon.

He ran on his toes down the walk. The chattering people let him through, shrinking a little when they saw his armament, but unwilling to impede him. When he came to the small, empty space where Shade and Armindez faced each other he paused. He did not step in between the two factions. He held the shotgun cradled under his left arm and dropped his right hand to his belt above the butt of the Colt.

He said, "That'll do it, Shade."

The headman for Morg Field turned, recognized him. He was helpless and behind him Frey and Halliday, experienced in the ways of Johnny Bracket now, hesitated. The man called "Swede," a large tow-head, swung up an arm and yelled, "It's only one, get to him!"

Johnny said, "Tell him, Shade."

The leader said, "Shut up, Swede."

Johnny said, "I don't know about the new people. But my men vote. Armindez, Diego, Manuelito, Jose and whoever else they say is local."

"You want a damn war right here?"

"I want what I say. And I want it quick. Otherwise, you may get your war. Only you won't be in it."

"You wouldn't shoot me, I'm not armed."

"No, I'd shoot Frey and Halliday and a few others. Seein' as you ain't armed, the mob would tear you apart."

Shade turned a trifle pale beneath his tan. "Mulloy should be here to handle this."

"Conspicuous by his absence, ain't he?"

"Him and Morg, this is their wagon," said Shade. "I ain't no lawman."

"Now, that's real nice, Shade," said Johnny. "You talked out of it real good. It just ain't your business."

He walked between the two factions then. He motioned for Armindez and his people to go through. He raised his hand and the others stopped, more curious than angry, waiting.

He addressed them in their own language and dialect, the Spanish of the southwest counties. He explained, laughing lightly, that Armindez and the others had proven themselves by establishing citizenship in this Territory and that in another year, come next May, they too could vote. This, he said, was a promise, Johnny Bracket promised them.

They called back to him, asking him what office he held, asking was he the "jefe," would he be running for boss next year, how did they know he was telling the truth?

He replied genially that they better had believe him because the last to call him a liar lay six feet beneath Texas soil. He was lying and they probably knew it, but they laughed, because he laughed. He knew they filed his promise away in their unforgetting minds, but they were with him now, and began to disperse, women and children first, then the men, returning quietly to the quarter set aside for them by the customs of the Territory in that day.

When they had gone and the Armindez faction had voted and it was quiet along the street, he still had not seen Mary, had not said more than a word to his friends. He was watching, waiting for trouble from Shade and the others. They were in The Four Aces and when the polls were closed they would get up enough nerve to start something, he thought.

He walked down to the bank. To his surprise Morg Field stood in the open doorway. Mulloy was behind him and in the bank, waiting attendance, was Randy Holt.

Johnny asked harshly, "And where were you when the trouble started?"

"Wasn't any trouble, thanks to you," said Morg Field.

"Thanks a lot for helping."

"Now, Johnny, that ain't smart. Supposin' Mulloy went down there official and someone started shootin'? You know them greasers."

Johnny said, "I don't call 'em greasers."

"Okay. But you know their hot temper. Mulloy goes down there, he has to take over, he's law. Best he should stay out of it. You did fine, Johnny, just fine."

He drew in a deep breath, looking at them. In the background Randy Holt's face was crimson, he shook his head violently in disagreement. Morg Field was smiling easily. Mulloy was expressionless.

Johnny said, "I swan to ginney. No wonder you get elected Mayor. You got butter runnin' out of your ears."

He turned and walked back toward the schoolhouse. It was time to talk with Mary and Lonely and Monty, now. There were matters to pore over. He had known Morg Field was smart, but he had underestimated the man. Now he saw the danger plain, as though written in fiery letters.

Few men can adjust so quickly, justify themselves so smoothly to circumstance, he thought. This is a man who would let the streets of his town run in blood and then claim innocence. By his own word he could set up riot, then disclaim responsibility. There was a man far more dangerous than any Johnny Bracket had ever known.

Morg Field was saying, "You can go home now, Holt. Everything is okay." He watched the young man hurry off. He went on, "Got to think about the Texan some more."

"He's damn mean."

"You note he didn't blow off at us."

"He may be damn smart, but I doubt it."

"You're sure about the Texas angle?"

"Old man Bracket didn't come there 'til long after we left," said Mulloy. "He minds his own business on his ranch. He's got him a young wife, good lookin', they say. Might keep that in mind."

"Let the Texas business stay put. Just so this Johnny doesn't know anything."

"He don't need to know anything, the way he slings his weight around. Amsy and Lonely and folks like that, they suck up to him."

"For once you put your finger on the nail head," said Morg Field. "That's why I have to do some thinkin' on him. That's the very reason."

He clapped Mulloy on the shoulder and they moved toward the schoolhouse where the counting was about concluded and where in a short space of time he would be acclaimed Mayor of the town he had taken over by cunning and strength.

From her window upstairs over The Four Aces, the woman watched everything that took place. Finally she saw Morg Field walking to his triumph, Tom Mulloy a respectful step behind. She quickly lowered the shade and went across to a cabinet of walnut which stood against the wall.

She opened a drawer and worked a hidden spring to reveal a false bottom. From it she took a blue bottle, common enough, but forsworn by her until quite lately. It contained laudanum in liquid form; she had brought it from San Francisco.

She took two wineglasses and filled one from a carafe. The other she poured half full, topping it with the drug. She drained this one, then sipped at the wine to ease the bitter taste.

Then she put away the blue bottle in its place of concealment and sat in a rocking chair. Its motion soothed her.

Johnny Bracket, she thought, is a man of impulse and sudden violence. I saw him kill the gambler, I saw him face down a mob. How can I use him without getting into trouble from which I will not escape?

It was something to get her teeth into while she slowly altered her love for Morg Field to hate. It was not that she wanted to stop loving him, it was that he would not allow it. This was intolerable. To be used without love was one thing, a matter of bargaining, so much for so much. To be used brutally, without feeling or compassion, by a man she had worshipped for his strength, it was not decent.

In the neat, well-lighted parlor there were Mary and Lonely and Monty and Amsy and Johnny and somehow they were all alike and together in this time. They talked and were agreed.

Amsy said, "It is going to be a great season for Morg Field and the bank. He has loaned to everyone within a hundred miles, at least on paper. Lately I understand little cash has changed hands, but it's a country of paper notes and no use going into that. There is early grass and what with interest and payments on the principle so that he can discount his own notes, he will make money and so will the people."

"Yes, it will be a prosperous summer. But when summer comes, can winter be far behind?" Lonely was getting ready to depart for the mountains. "The man is as dangerous as a bed of rattlers."

"He is," said Johnny Bracket, noting how Monty said nothing, but sat looking at Mary, not blaming the Britisher.

"I wish you wouldn't see so much of him, Mary."

She laughed. "Admitting all you say is true, why shouldn't I see him and listen to his boasting?"

"Ah, well . . . that," said Johnny. Yet she had told them nothing, taking no part in the examination of Morg and that for which he stood and the way he was. "But he's bad, you know. Real bad. I didn't realize it until today, when he gave me the false laugh and his tongue dripped lies. I had thought here was a man on the make, so what? The world is full of them, they run the country, all countries. I thought I'd go along for the ride and maybe do something for myself I've never been able to do before."

"And what else can you do now?" Mary asked.

"Nothin'," said Lonely. "He can't do anything but go out yonder and make the ranch strong and proper."

"Lay low and raise cattle," said Amsy Buchanan. "Time will come when you get free of him."

"I owe him the money fair and square," Johnny told them. "I got to go my own way and pay him back."

Mary went out on the porch and in a moment conversation died and he joined her there. They sat together on a bench in darkness and she put her hand on his.

"I'll be careful . . . with Morg."

He said, "Love is a curious animal, ain't it?"

She melted closer to him. "I'm very new at it."

"Me too," he confessed. He knew what to do with his hands but he was afraid to begin. She lay in the circle of his left arm.

She said, "I think you ought to kiss me. Tomorrow you will be gone and Grandpa will be gone prospecting and I shall be very lonely."

His arm tightened as she turned up her face. He could not see her, he only knew her eyes were closed and her lips parted. Their quick breath intermingled and then he knew what to do with his hands and it was all right because she wanted to be touched and caressed.

# chapter seven

IT WAS A summer of vast content and great progress. The fall round-up promised a burgeoning herd, the home ranch was shiny and four square and Monty did not take a drink throughout the hottest of dog days. Johnny Bracket was, for the first time in his life, almost completely happy.

Tom Mulloy dropped by, wiped sweat from his brow, drank deeply from the well, fingered his moustache and said, "Finest water this side o' hell. You're doin' good, Johnny."

"Not doin' bad yourself. Hear you got a shipment of prime stock last week."

"Yeah. I got Moriarty and Swede out there, now." Mulloy shook his head. "I'm a city fella. Ranchin' is for country boys. Morg got me into it, to start with."

"It's good cattle country. Morg was right."

"Oh, he's right as rain. Never seen him when he wasn't." Mulloy grinned, showing uneven teeth. "He's makin' 'em toe the mark in town since he's Mayor."

"I heard." Johnny did not add to this. He saw Mulloy's sly acknowledgement of words unsaid and was glad when the Marshal turned away.

"See you in the calaboose," said the town's officer as he mounted and rode down the trail. Just before he was out of sight Rag Shade came down the hill and joined him. In a moment or two Halliday and Frey fell into line behind the others.

Monty came from the corral, cramming tobacco into a pipe. He looked after the riders and smiled. "Circle F and X-Y ride awfully close, eh, Johnny?"

"None of our business."

"Right-o."

"On t' other hand," said Johnny, "X-Y is gettin' a lot of re-branded stuff from the south."

"Which also is not our affair?"

"Right-o," said Johnny.

Monty struck a sulphurous match, watched it flame, ap-

60

plied it to the tobacco in the briar. "Spell it out, old boy, will you?"

"Can't do that. Just guessin'. I'd say Shade and the others spend a lot of time off the home range, which is Circle F. Field's got a big herd. Mulloy's X-Y is gettin' to be almost as big, but Mulloy's heart ain't in raisin' cattle. Morg Field's got some kinda idea which we can't know and shouldn't even guess."

"There have been complaints from the south. Threats of hanging the first rustler caught in the act."

"We ain't stealin' any beef and we ain't hangin' nor about to be hanged," said Johnny. "We're doin' right well as it is. Like I wrote Pa, the goose hangs high."

"And fat," agreed Monty. "I had better begin dinner arrangements for the men." He walked toward the house, a mild-speaking, stocky, careful man. He had assumed the duties of cook when the outdoor work was in hand, and no one could do it better. It was never necessary to mention anything more than once to Monty. He was the most satisfactory kind of man to have around.

Johnny went to his pony, saddled and ready, mounted and rode out to the north. He had hired Jim Banning, a drifter but a good cattle man, to work two local Mexican vaqueros named Cantero and Silvy for the season. Banning was a leathery, taciturn man with dewlaps like a basset hound, a veteran of many ranges.

The three were sitting their mounts atop the hill two miles in back of the home ranch. They were looking east toward the X-Y when Johnny rode up to them.

"Boss," said Banning, "howdy."

Johnny said mildly, "Shouldn't you all be up at Red Canyon?"

"We got the stuff outa the canyon."

"Good. Anything else?"

The vaqueros, unsmiling, saluted and rode off toward the west pasture. Banning sat, hat tipped low over his eyes.

Johnny said, "You might's well spit it out."

"Yeah," Banning lifted his head. He had wide-spaced eyes, squinted and greenish. He spat tobacco juice downwind. "Yeah, Boss. Heard a shot up yonder whilst we was workin' the cattle. The boys spooked a little. You know how they are since the Mayor's been clampin' down on the spick citizens."

Johnny said, "I'm a great one for minding my own business."

"Yeah," said Banning. "Well, I heard those shots."

"Uh-huh. And then?"

"I rode over to keep the men quiet. You know. They get rattled, they're no good with the cattle."

"That's right."

"I was too late to see it all." He paused. "You know Deep Canyon?"

"Sure, I know Deep Canyon." It was a wide crack in the foothills, a freak of nature, seemingly bottomless, a fissure created by a long ago earthquake.

"Shade and his pair was ridin' away from it on the opposite side from me. They waved real polite. Mulloy was on my side of the canyon, ridin' hell bent thisaway. Now it don't make sense Shade and his were firin' at Mulloy or vicey versa, does it?"

"Go on, Banning."

"There was a horse, runnin' free, on Shade's side."

"Yes?" Banning was worried, Johnny saw, deeply concerned.

"I went down into Deep Canyon. Took me quite a piece of time and some trouble."

"I've been down there."

"Then you know."

"What did you find?"

"Man I used to know. Name of Gilhooley. He was shot and he was still warm."

"What about Gilhooley?"

"Trouble is, Boss, I don't know what about Gilhooley. He's one of those you never can tell about."

"A sometimes man?"

"Yeah. I known him to swing a wide loop. I known him to be a deputy."

Johnny said, "Was he carrying a badge?"

"No. He wasn't carrying anything. I figure they shot him, then dumped him in the canyon."

"You figure it's our business?"

Banning asked, "Are we part of it?"

"We ain't part of anything except this particular ranch and what's on it."

Banning looked at the horizon, then at the ground. He said, "All right, Boss. We mind our own business."

He mounted his pony and rode after the hired hands.

Johnny turned back toward the house. There was nothing he could do about Gilhooley, dead in Deep Canyon. The man may have been caught red-handed by Shade and the others, running an iron on some Field or Mulloy cattle. He might have stolen the horse Banning had reported running free.

He did not believe nor disbelieve. He had no axe to grind for the ranchers southward nor for Field nor Mulloy. He felt no moral duty toward the man in the gorge because Banning had said he was a part time thief. Sooner or later they all came to their end in some cul-de-sac. It was a hard world in the West in this time, he thought. His own affairs lay close to home, where he had to prepare to make a mortgage payment by next springtime. The summer was going fine, nobody was giving him any trouble.

He had to stay clear. Nobody had elected him to office, he wasn't a lawman, had never been one, didn't ever intend being one. That was for his brother, Sam Bracket. Sometimes it was for Toole Bracket, but never for Johnny. He was a cattleman and meant to remain one.

Still, he was uneasy, going about small tasks in the tack room they had built into the house, hearing Monty in the kitchen, waiting for the end of another long day. There was always a tomorrow and it was necessary to figure what it might be like and which way a man had to go when the chips were down. Morg Field was pushing at the Mexican-Americans and Rag Shade was a killer and probably a thief and Mulloy was Field's man and the town was completely under Morg's control.

There were no other ranches nearby, only Circle F, X-Y and this place. No one else had been able to make it here in the short space of time since Field had brought in the first herd. There was a row of rocky, mean foothills to the south which isolated the country from neighbors—with a couple of arroyos through which stolen beef might be driven at night, he added to himself.

He decided that he was brooding too much, that he had been away from town—and Mary—for too long. He rode back to the house and announced that he was going, giving no reason, acknowledging Monty's smile and wave with a nod.

In the back room of the bank Morg Field listened and

was silent. On his desk was a nickel-plated star and a poke with a few dollars in it.

"He was a lawman," said Shade defensively. "I backtracked on him. He took a shot at me."

"All right," said Field. "I heard you the first time."

"I wouldn't of done anything if he hadn't gunned me."

Field sighed and put the star in his desk drawer. "It wasn't your fault. And dumpin' him in Deep Canyon was smart, Rag. Only thing, you say Bracket's foreman saw you?"

"That was after we got rid of the lawman. His saddle, too. We'll put our brand on his hoss tomorrow."

"You should have done it today."

"Wasn't time, Morg," said Shade. "Banning come up before we could unlimber an iron."

"All right," said Field again. He didn't like it, but there was nothing to be done about it now. "So long as the cattle are fixed okay."

"Nobody can cut a brand like me, you know that."

"Ear vents the same?"

Shade grinned. "We don't take none that ain't like yours."

"Okay." Morg put a hundred dollars on the desk top. "You and the boys better stay sober this trip."

Shade picked up the money. "I see what you mean. I'll manage 'em."

"Maybe you'd like to put some of that extra money in the bank," Field suggested. "May come a time it'll be handy."

Shade shook his head. "That time comes, I want it handier than that, Morg."

Field laughed. "That time won't come while you work for me."

"I don't reckon it will. But you can't teach an old dog. I'll hang onto my share. The boys, well, they won't."

"That's why you're foreman, Rag." Field stood up and winked in a friendly manner. Shade went out feeling that he had done his duty.

Field sat down again, scowling. One slip, he thought, one hole in the operation, and word would go to Territorial headquarters and the Cattleman's Association would be on him like a pack of wolves. Just one slip, like if Rag had been careless and buried the range detective instead of dumping him into Deep Canyon. Bodies could be dug up. Men like Banning could bear witness. Johnny Bracket . . . you never knew how Johnny stood. He seemed to go along, but he got horsey about his friends in the Mex quarter, he asked questions when he should be keeping his mouth shut. And . . . he kept hanging around Mary Jones.

There was a discreet tap on the rear door. Morg arose, went from behind his desk and operated a small Judas hole. Then he opened the door, frowning a little as Susan Carter came in and smiled at him.

"It's all right," she said. "I looked both ways before I came through the gate in the fence. No one saw me."

"That ain't the point. This is business hours."

"Just go tell that nice Randy Holt you don't want to be disturbed. That's what you always have done."

She sat on a straight chair. She was wearing a light grey dress from San Francisco, cut very low. Her dark skin shone a little beneath the light flecking of powder. Her perfume gave the cigar smoke competition in the small room. Her eyes could have been mocking, except that he knew she dared not mock him.

"I don't have to hide," he said. She was beautiful, all right, but lately she could discompose him. He had tried hurting her, but it no longer seemed to work. She accepted his abuses without crying out—that damned Indian in her. She never bothered to reprove him for his outbursts, although she must have guessed what was in her future.

"Of course not," she agreed. "I just saw Bracket."

"What of it?" There could only be one reason she mentioned it, he knew. He kept his face expressionless as possible; it was one thing he could not, would not discuss with her.

"He was whispering in a very pretty ear," she said, lifting a shoulder so that her breasts moved one against the other beneath the lace. There was a time when this would have roused him, now he only felt fatigue and annoyance.

He said, "Any more local gossip? I didn't know you got around so much. You didn't useta."

"I see much through my window. A gallery seat, but mine own. I wonder if I might not have a trip, Morg."

"San Francisco? Back to that?"

"Oh, no. I thought maybe Denver. The new hotel—they say it's very fine."

He thought a moment, then brightened. "You know, that is a good idea. You probably got cabin fever. Sittin' up there alone, so much."

"Yes. Cabin fever." She put a hand to her face to conceal her immediate concern at his ready agreement. "I thought maybe some dinners, a shopping spree."

He took out the thick wallet and passed over most of its contents. "Have I ever denied you?"

"No, Morg. You're always good with the money."

He said, "I've still got plans for us, y' know."

"Yes. You have plans."

"That's what got me where I am. Makin' plans, big plans."

"It surely has," she said. She feared any plan he now had for her. She determined to carry her derringer in her reticule this trip, to keep it near her every moment, sleeping and waking. She picked up the money. "I can leave on the evening train."

"So soon?" He smiled widely upon her. "Anxious to be quit of me?"

"You know better than that." She kissed him quickly and went to the door. "Don't be careless, now. Keep making those plans come true."

She smiled at him and departed.

He sat down again behind the desk. Johnny Bracket, he thought, in town during the workaday week. Just to see Mary Jones; of course, it had to be that way. Well, something had to be done, but in due time, without haste.

He bit furiously at the end of another cigar.

It was a summer of many diversions. Field City played a baseball game against Territorial City. Johnny was the catcher and Monty distinguished himself by striking out twelve opponents with a sidearm adaptation of a cricketer's bowling motion. A pair of vagrants tried to hold up the bank and were shot by Mulloy and the Swede, after which a wandering photographer snapped the dead men all stretched out in the afternoon sunshine. The pictures were still on display in the window of the bank.

Lonely Jones found the desert immeasurably hot and took to prying around in the mountains behind Johnny's ranch, stopping in now and then for food and talk. Susan Carter returned from Denver arrayed like a lily of the field and twice smiled invitingly upon Johnny. He was slightly tempted, but found strength in his "understanding" with Mary Jones.

Eighteen babies were born in the Mexican quarter, each bringing on a celebration which caused friction with the authorities, but no bones were broken. Morgan Field loaned money to everyone and anyone in anticipation of the fall market for the cattle which grew in every grass-rich pasture.

And then it was autumn, but no ordinary season. The sun faded fast, far too fast. Frost came in early October before there was any shipping. The prices in the East had suddenly tumbled, everyone was holding onto his beef for a rise.

And then the first blizzard hit, six weeks too early for any possible preparation. Barns were inadequate, home pastures soon overstocked with lowing, complaining beeves. There were losses up and down the Territory and in Johnny Bracket there was a premonition. Things had been going along too well.

The second blizzard came in early November. Underneath its white coat was the slush of the first storm, which now froze hard, killing the grass of an Indian summer which never came.

One snowfall followed the other, with freezing winds coming down from the north. Men worked wet and cold, came down with pneumonia, died trying to keep cattle alive. Young trees were eaten, swollen bellies littered the white fields. Cattle perished by the tens of thousands, first the calves, then the cows carrying calves, then the bulls. There was little anyone could do but watch the loss of his herds.

Johnny Bracket fared better than most. His pastures lay in close, he had the barn in which to keep his breeders and one fine young bull. Monty was invaluable in knowing how and where to provide temporary shelter for a few head which remained close to the buildings. Banning found fodder in the high places where the mountains provided bare spots for winter foliage to live.

Christmas at the Jones' house in town was dismal, yet Mary and Johnny found a moment alone, when woes were forgotten over Tom and Jerry made with rye whiskey.

She said, "Can't you sell, Johnny? Morg is shipping."

He shook his head. "At the market price, I'd lose money. I can't get them in and they wouldn't weigh out. The stock I've got safe will breed up for the future. Only the big holders can afford to sell so cheap."

Lonely overheard and came across the room to join them. "Johnny's right. There's somethin' wrong with cattle prices back East. It's a bad year. If you can stick it out with your stockers, you'll be all right, boy."

Mary said, "What's going to happen to the others?"

"It's up to Morg," said Johnny. "Everybody in the county owes the bank."

"And the good Lord help 'em," said Lonely, moving back to the punch bowl.

"It's to Morg's interest to keep the county prosperous," said Johnny. "Otherwise, where'll he get his profits?"

"You know Pa," she said, frowning. "He can't see anything but bad in Morg."

They talked of other things and then Morg Field himself appeared, laden with gifts for everyone. There was a pearl necklace for Mary.

She let him fasten the clasp and surveyed herself in the mirror. Johnny stood back—he had managed a small ring set with a diamond chip and it flashed when she touched the pearls.

She said, "They're lovely, Morg, but I can't accept them."

"That's pretty funny," said Morg. His heavy features were sullen as his eye caught the tiny diamond. "How come all of a sudden you can't take a little present from an old friend?"

She removed the necklace and extended it to him. "We have a little announcement. Grandpa?"

Lonely lifted his mug of Tom and Jerry. "Everybody fill up."

Monty moved among them, refilling the cups. Twice he paused, looked longingly at the punch bowl, each time he was able to grin and continue to serve without sampling.

Morg Field's features had reassembled, he was clutching a tall glass full of the white liquid. Once he glanced at Johnny, then quickly looked away.

Lonely teetered on his toes, beaming around the room. Pedro and Consuela were there and Banning and several townsfolk. It was late afternoon and the sun had not shone in weeks. The Christmas tree stood in a corner, proud and tall and gay with paper rings and tinsel angels and popcorn strung from branch to branch.

Lonely said, "I'm right proud to tell you all, my daughter, Mary, has—uh—plighted her troth. Here's to the future groom—Johnny Bracket."

There was quick babble. No one was surprised, Johnny thought, not even Morg. They flocked around him, wringing his hand, slapping his back. Mary stood beside him, her head high, flushing a little, but composed. Morg came last, his drink in his left hand.

"Congratulations, Johnny. The better man wins again."

"Thank you, Morg, but better or worse is the way it reads," he answered. "Nobody knows until the chips are down who's best."

Morg said, "Good thing to remember." He touched Mary's hand, did not look at her. He went on, spoke with other people, a thickset, strong man, the air of authority more pronounced, Johnny thought. Then he stared at Johnny once more and abruptly took his departure.

Lonely said in Johnny's ear, "Now you got a hiyu, number one enemy, son."

"You may be right, at that."

"You seen him, the way he looked?"

"I saw him."

"You got any doubts whatsoever?"

Johnny thought a moment, then said, "It's like this, Lonely, when a man hates he has to do somethin'. When a smart man hates, he bides his time. I'll wait and see what this man tries to do to me."

"You won't have long," said Lonely. "Just until springtime, when the payment's due on the quarterly interest."

"Morg's got his money to protect," said Johnny. "I'm a good investment."

"Like you say, son, wait and see."

What else could he do, Johnny wondered, but hang tough? He had been committed with the land. Now he was involved to the end, life or death. He turned and Mary caught his hand and held it.

# chapter eight

MARY JONES RODE to the top of the hill outside town and dismounted from one of Amsy Buchanan's hack ponies. A bird sang and she was grateful. Springtime had come to the county and the sun shone as though no bitterness of winter had existed so recently.

She seldom rode any more; she was busy with a hundred

small plans for the wedding. She was to be married in June, very early in the month of brides, and nothing else seemed to be important. She had dismissed school early that afternoon, knowing Johnny was out on the range, wanting to be alone.

She thought about the ranch and how the house was being beautifully rebuilt and rearranged by Monty. He was making furniture to fit her own wishes, painting and paperhanging. There would be no house like it in the Valley—in the Territory.

She thought about Johnny, how tender-tough, how good, how uncompromising. She wondered about his family, of whom he spoke so often as time went on. She had written to his father, but as yet there had been no reply. She hoped they would all come for the wedding.

These were simple, surface thoughts, which today was what she wanted to let run through her mind. There were other, deeper ruminations which she buried: worriment about her increasing physical response to Johnny; wonderment about her grandfather and his prolonged absence this spring; remembrances of her father, that idealistic dreamer who had bequeathed a certain unworldliness to his only child, herself.

Lonely was unerringly correct about the latter. In Mary there was a lot of her father, who had founded a town and then been unable to foster it. She could well recall his aimless meanderings, his talk of socialistic community, of the brotherhood of man in bloom here amidst the western wilderness. He had thought to find gold in the hills and to use it to provide plenty for one and all. She could remember how his eyes gleamed, and how little he had done to make his erratic planning come to fruition.

Then Morg Field had come and soon her father was dead. It was no fight, there had been no clash. Before the ruthless, whirlwind tactics of Morg he had been hapless and helpless. She could find no excuse for him, he was a bewildered weakling among men of purpose and strength.

Still, there was something of her father in her. There was a detachment, broken only by the advent of Johnny Bracket. She had always been cool, a thinker but a pragmatist, believing in compromise, rebelling against idealism but allowing time and events to pass her by. Even now, she had these deep inner doubts. Could she be a good wife? Was Johnny the right man? Wasn't her grandfather an old fool to continually attempt to fight Morg?

When Morg Field rode up on his black stallion, and sat looking down at her, she was not surprised. It was as if he had stepped fully armed from her thoughts.

He said, "Saw you come out this way. Figured you'd be up here, enjoyin' the view."

"It's a lovely view."

He got down, light on his feet for a big man, and stood beside her. The town lay like a checkerboard below them.

He said directly, "It's a good town. Your daddy founded it, I made it go."

"How many times have I heard that from you, Morg?"

"It's true."

"Partly true."

"All the way true. If he had lived, we would have built together."

She said, "That's nonsense and you know it."

"Maybe I wanted it that way." His tone changed and she moved uneasily apart from him. "Mary . . . you're not goin' to marry Bracket, are you?"

She felt a slight shock. Did Morg know her well enough to sense the deep, inner doubts? "Are you crazy?"

His big hand gripped her elbow, almost lifting her from her booted feet. "You can't marry him. You know how I feel. You know I've wanted to ask you to marry me."

"Let go, Morg," she said.

"I been bidin' my time, waiting for the right chance," he said, pulling her toward him.

She retorted, "Until you could get rid of Susan Carter?"

"I'll send her away tomorrow. Just say you won't marry Bracket and I'll put her on the night train."

She shook herself free. She faced him, feet planted apart. She was angry, now. "You dare to say a thing like that to me? You think I'd bargain with you?"

"You don't have to promise to marry me. Just that you won't marry him."

She said, "I always knew you had a devious mind, Morg. I never thought you'd come at me like this. It's disgusting. Now, will you go away and leave me alone?"

He grabbed at her. She was supple and strong and very quick. She was wearing a divided skirt and riding boots and when she kicked him in the shins, she knew it hurt him.

The struggle became ridiculous in a matter of moments and he sensed it and stood away, breathing hard.

She said, "Now you see, it is over. I mean that any friendship between us is ended. I didn't want it that way. I've admired some things in you. You've spoiled everything."

The blackness was on him. He took a big stride toward her. Then he stopped, his teeth showing, his eyes sunken, hands opening and closing. He spoke in a low, choked voice, "I've spoiled it? By touching you? What do you think life is made of, you school marm?"

"Of you and Susan Carter," she said harshly. "And of Mulloy and Rag Shade and men like them. You and my father! That's very funny, when you stop and think of it. You shouldn't be mentioned in the same breath."

"That's damn right," he shouted. "Your father and Johnny Bracket. Good men. You want to live your life with good men? You're a fool, Mary. There's more to you than that."

"If there is, you'll never know it," she snapped. She turned and untied her horse and mounted, vaulting into the saddle like a boy. She rode breakneck down the hill toward town.

He stood there, choking back the rage which he had not turned loose for many a year, not since coming to the Territory. She rode magnificently, her booted heels slapping at the pony's sides. He wanted her, wanted to marry her, she was everything he desired in the world.

The fact that he couldn't have her twisted his guts, so that he cursed in a low monotone, slamming his fist against the bark of the tree.

He gained control. He shifted his thoughts to Johnny Bracket. Now he could think coolly and calmly. Here was a matter he could handle. This was something he knew all about, how to take care of meddling outsiders.

He could let the anger and hatred flow into a nice, narrow channel, thinking about Bracket. He could make plans and carry them out with despatch. He was gentle with the bridle of the black horse, mounting. He rode out in the direction of Circle F where Rag Shade would be waiting orders while the other riders worked the springtime range for what poor specimens were to be found after the hard winter.

He had come out of it pretty well. Of course he had lost money, but everyone else was worse off and this was what counted because power was better than hard cash. He held paper, mortgages, easily turned into liens. So long as the balance of power was in his grasp he could afford to lose cash profits. Tomorrow's gain would more than make it up.

Riding onto Circle F property his satisfaction grew. The gradual slope of ground already showed the tender shoots of early grass. He held high gun, he controlled the water at its source. When he turned into the lane which led to the ranch house he was in normal spirits.

Rag Shade was in the kitchen, worrying Yung Low, the Chinese cook, a skinny little oriental with an evil temper. Morg called him out into the waning afternoon. They sat on the top rail of the corral fence watching the black stallion flare his nostrils at a small dun mare.

"Boys comin' in early?"

"Yeah," said Shade. "Nothin' much to do since we shipped. That is, until we go south again."

"That will be awhile, yet. My man down there says we got to lay low. They got the Association roused."

"That was an Association man we dumped into Deep Canyon."

"Yes," said Field. "Mulloy stalled them good on him. But never mind that. We're ridin' over to Bracket's place when the boys come in."

"I been waitin' for that."

"You been real patient. Just hold off a little longer."

"You mean it ain't time to kill a Texan?"

Field looked at his foreman. "You're pretty sure of yourself, Rag."

"Me? Why, boss, I been around. I seen him draw, I been hit by him. He's poison. But you know, I never did see the man who could take a bullet in the back and not be hurt."

"Yeah," said Field. "I'm glad you got common sense enough to play it right. We're goin' to break him, is what we're goin' to do. We're goin' to run him off and then you can have him on the way out."

"'Scuse me for livin', but did I hear you say we're goin' to run him off?"

"Legally, Rag, legally. Not with guns."

"Boss, you goin' over there and tell him that?"

"As soon as the boys come in."

"Then I better get busy." The foreman went across to the wall and took down his rifle. He took a bottle of oil and a rag from a shelf. "I want a clean gun when we go against this Texan."

Field was amused. "You have more respect for him than I thought."

"Respect, that I got. Scared of him, I ain't. He's a sudden man, and you got to be ready for that kind."

It was good to see the manner in which Shade responded. It proved that Morg had not hired the wrong man for the job. It balanced things out. There were more ways than one to skin a coyote, and Rag was ready for the last and hardest way and that was good.

Frey and Halliday came in. They ate hastily, refried beans and steak, swallowed coffee and were out in the gathering dark for the Jenkins place.

Morg Field rode into the reflected light from the windows of the rebuilt ranch house and announced himself in a loud, confident tone. The door opened and he went toward the veranda. Johnny Bracket blinked past him and asked, "Your boys comin' in, too?"

"They'll wait," said Morg. "Don't reckon to be long, this visit."

"Oh?" Bracket seemed puzzled.

Inside the house, Morg Field felt himself again growing too angry. It was too plainly apparent that this was a place being readied for a bride. Monty Carruthers was hanging curtains at the kitchen window, ruffled bits of material made of hard linen. Through an open door he could see the bed, canopied, with a fine-stitched coverlet. He could not go through with the sham heartiness he had intended.

He said, "Monty, how are you?" He turned to Bracket. "Bad news, Johnny. The eastern bankers are callin' notes on me."

"That's real bad." Johnny hesitated. "I'll have the interest money and a payment for you next week. I'm takin' a beatin', but I sold enough beef to make out."

"Afraid it won't do."

There was a pause in the room, a significant alteration of attitudes.

"I guess you'll have to speak plainer, Morg."

"I got to tell you right out," Morg agreed. "I'll want the whole sum."

"It ain't due."

"You didn't read the tiny writin'," said Field. "After six months it is due upon demand. I wrote it myself, Johnny."

Again the silence. Johnny walked across the room, then

back to the table. There was a lamp on it, with a store bought pretty green shade. He sat down so that the light fell on his hard hands, folded before him.

"So, that's the ticket, huh, Morg?"

Monty inhaled in the background, pausing in his task. Morg Field loomed, standing near the door.

"There's a panic on back East," said Morg Field. "They got me in the middle. I can sell this place, make enough to help tide me over."

"That's a damn lie and you know it." Johnny's voice did not alter, he spoke clearly and simply.

Now that the issue was well joined, Morg Field felt easier, more in control of himself. He smiled, "I wouldn't take that talk from anyone but you. I'm sorry, like I say, but you've got thirty days to come up with the full sum, plus the interest. Anyone in town will agree that I'm givin' you fair notice in front of your own witness. No use startin' anything, Johnny."

Johnny said thoughtfully, "The place is worth at least ten thousand just as she stands. Monty and me made it valuable. In another year it'll be worth twenty-five thousand. If it hadn't been for the bad winter, I could have paid you off. I got to admit, Morg, you're a shrewd businessman."

"Look, if I had the money I'd let the mortgage ride. I've told a dozen people in town that very fact."

"Sure, you have. You're all kinds of smart."

"You think yours is the only loan I got to call? I'm bein' pushed, I got to collect cash." He was enjoying himself now, pointing out the ramifications of his schemes, showing Bracket how he could not escape the web.

"Uh-huh. You sure got it nailed down. Only—I ain't playin' your game."

Morg said, "Run that past me again, Johnny?"

"Well, I just ain't leavin'. You want me to get out inside thirty days. You want me to worry and stew and then just ride out. I won't do it."

Morg said, "You'll fight the law?"

"Tom Mulloy? His deputies? Your boys?"

"The courts'll have something to say."

"Territorial courts? They're fine. But they don't convene too often, nor too soon," said Johnny. "Then you still got to serve papers."

"Now look, you can't fight the law."

"I can fight for what's right," said Johnny quietly. "I can go in and tell my side of it, then I can shoot any son who tries to occupy my land. You want a range war. You can have it."

"Now, look here, I'm tryin' to do this legal and right."

"You're tryin' to do it legal and shyster-right," said Johnny. He got up and went across the room and reached down his rifle. He tucked the Colts in his waistband.

For a minute Morg Field was afraid. He edged toward the door, his eyes on the Texan.

Then Johnny said, "Monty, put out the light."

Monty came to blow out the lamp. In the darkness, Johnny said, "Lesson number one: I ain't about to be sky-lined by your little gun-toters, Morg. Lesson number two, for homework: Don't come back here with any more of your threats or arguments. A last word: Get the hell out and get out fast."

"We been friends," said Morg Field. "I'm sorry as all hell about this." His voice was loud and carrying as he opened the door. "It ain't goin' to look good nor sound good around town."

Shade's voice came from the gloom, "Everything all right, boss?"

Johnny answered, "Just fine, Shade. You take your boss-man and nurse him careful. He's all in one piece, for now."

Shade snapped, "You answer me, Morg."

"I'm all right," said Field. He walked down the steps and across the yard to his horse. "It's Bracket who's in trouble. I'll be seein' you folks." He mounted. "Nice house you've fixed up there. It'll make good headquarters for me."

He wheeled the stallion too quickly and the horse reared. He brought a big fist down between the beast's ears, sending the forefeet back to earth, taming it. He rode off in a thunder of hard hoofs. The three men waited a moment then Halliday and Frey followed.

Rag Shade called, "Got me covered, huh, Bracket?"

"You want a showdown, just you and me?"

"Hell, no, I'm just storin' up things for you. When my time comes, you won't be holdin' no gun on me."

"That's the way she figures," said Johnny with a cheerfulness he was far from feeling. "Run along with your bad old bossman. Be seein' you when you got your guts with you."

"I got guts enough," said Shade without rancour. "I also take lessons in bein' smart. From old bossman."

He rode down the trail toward the main road.

Johnny went back into the house. Monty put down the light hunting rifle he had been holding. They did not relight the lamp; they sat at the table in darkness and silence.

From without a familiar voice said, "They've gone. You can rest easy."

"Lonely!"

The old prospector came in the rear door and through the kitchen. Monty struck a sulphur match. The warm glow spread through the room as Lonely removed an ancient and battered hat to join them at the table.

"Howdy, gents."

"You get in on the grand ball?"

"Yep."

Monty said hesitatingly, "He was waiting for them, Johnny. Asked me not to mention it."

"How did you know they were coming?"

Lonely said, "I been expecting it for awhile. To be exact, since Christmas."

"Yes. Since Christmas." No need to mention Mary. They all knew.

Lonely said, "He's got you over a barrel."

"He has, you know," said Monty.

"I know. I was bluffin'."

"You could hold out awhile. But if you check with the people in town, you'll know he's got you."

"It was damn smart," Johnny acknowledged. "I should have read the mortgage more careful."

"Nobody ever does. Howsomever," Lonely went on, "this county's needed a man for some time."

"Not a dumbhead like me."

"An honest dumbhead is better'n a smart thief. Like the way I figured Morg was headin' this way, a young fella named Randy Holt has been keepin' me informed what stews in the bank."

"Holt? The young squirt who's always moonin' over Mary?"

"Lucky for us, he always has been like that about Mary. Well, anyway, part of what he says is true. Money is awful tight. Back East is worse. The town knows it, they can't fault him for closin' on properties."

"And he can bring in guns enough to run me off. Any more good news?"

"Straight facts. And a little old fashioned skulduggery," said Lonely, "is what I got in mind."

Monty said, "Listen to him, Johnny. He has got it, I think."

"I'm all ears," said Johnny. "I'm stupid, but I know enough to listen to my elders."

"My son called the town down there by a good name. 'Hope City.' Then he couldn't produce hope for the people. Morg Field did . . . By the way, did you know he came from Texas? El Paso, I believe."

"Texas is another place."

"Right," replied Lonely. "Just thought I'd mention it. Well, Morg's a crook. I believe he's a killer. Only as we all know, he's smart."

"Smart enough to fool a whole town, a county, maybe the Territory."

"Yep. Only maybe we can figure to outsmart him. I had some luck this year. I brought in some dust." He casually tossed a heavy bag onto the table. "Got it over beyond the Padres."

"Why that's fine, Lonely. That's real fine. You got quite a stake there."

"There's another bag in the creek."

"Over in the Padres?"

"Nope. Right up in back of you. Maybe twenty mile. Off-shoot of your own water. Call it Picayune Creek."

"Well, why don't you pan it out?"

"On account of I put it in."

"You did what?"

"Salted the Picayune."

"But why, for Heaven's sake?"

Lonely's faded blue eyes twinkled. "You ever heard of saltin' a creek, son?"

"Sure, everybody has."

"After it was found out, they heard of it. You ever see a gold rush?"

"I don't follow you."

Lonely said, "Elections are comin' up again. Jarret against Field. Only I've had some talks with Jarret. He owes the bank. He's beginning to see the light."

Johnny said, "I still don't get it."

"Bring in some people. The man at the telegraph office, Steering, he's one of Morg's. Supposin' we sent for supplies?

Supposin' you wired your own folks, down Texas, said there was gold, they should come and get it?"

Johnny said, "A gold rush would bring confusion, all right. And we need time."

Lonely said, "Just thought I'd check before I put this poke into the creek."

"Mulloy couldn't handle a gold rush crowd. He'd be easy for them to bribe. The town would go dirty. You want the town to suffer, Lonely?"

"The town suffers Morg Field. Let it pay a little to get him off its back," said Lonely. "Got to fight fire with fire."

Johnny sat back on his chair. Monty, he saw, would go along with the idea. For a moment he wondered what Mary would say, then he knew it was not Mary's decision, that it was up to the three of them here, in this room.

Monty said, "Not quite honest, but then, what about Mr. Field, eh?"

"I dunno," said Johnny. "I just don't know."

"Get things stirred up, we might manage a hand hold," said Lonely. "You got any better idea?"

"No," said Johnny. "I haven't got a smidgin of an idea."

"Sleep on it," said Lonely. "I'm stickin' around until you say. My son—he wasn't big enough nor tough enough. And I liked that name, Hope City. This is a chance, maybe an outside chance, to bring back Hope City."

They all sat quietly, each with his own thoughts. The lamp sputtered, but no one noticed.

## chapter nine

MARY JONES STOOD with Amsy Buchanan in a shadow thrown by the night lamp of the livery stable. She said, "I must be getting home. It's late. But I did want to talk with you about the election."

"We've got 'em lined up," said Amsy. "If we can vote the Mexican-Americans, I believe we'll make a showing."

"They will vote if we can show strength."

"It's up to Johnny and Sime Jarret. Johnny can handle the gunmen. If Jarret holds true, we can beat Morg."

There was a clatter of hoofs. Four riders came into the stable yard too fast, skidded to a stop. She heard Morg's heavy voice and moved deeper into the shadow. Amsy went forward into the light.

Shade and the other two riders were already unsaddling, turning their mounts into the public corral. Morg led his stallion toward the barn. Amsy intercepted him, offering to take over.

"I hear you don't like the way I'm runnin' this town," she heard Morg say in an ugly voice she had never heard him use before.

"Politics is politics," Amsy answered reasonably.

"And you're messin' with the damn greasers to get votes, too. I'm warnin' you, Amsy, they'll never get to the polls. We almost had it last year. This time it'll be curtains."

"For them and me, too? Is that what you mean?"

"For anybody that tries to vote 'em," said Morg.

"That's somethin' I got to see," Amsy told him.

She saw Shade and the other pair come toward the stable. She saw Amsy face them. Morg looked as though he was ready to kill someone on the spot.

"You may not live to see it, stableman," Shade said.

Amsy stepped back from horse and men. He was patently unarmed. He showed no fear. He said, "No jackleg hired gun is going to do anything about it, Shade."

Shade stepped forward, feinted with a left and hit Amsy in the jaw. The aging liveryman staggered back against the wall. Shade went in on him, punching.

Mary came running. She went past Morg, grabbed Shade by the elbow, screaming.

Shade fell back, ready to throw a punch, then staring in disbelief as Mary slapped hard at his face. He looked at Morg, hands at his sides, lifting a shoulder.

Field said, "You too, Mary. You're with them."

"One hundred and ten per cent," she said. "One thousand per cent. You and your dirty bullies! Shame on you! I hope you rot, you lowdown, miserable cowards!"

For a moment it seemed Field would attack her. Then he dropped a heavy arm and said, "Come on, boys, the drinks are on me."

She held Amsy's head on her knee as they swaggered out of the yard. She raised him, supported him to the house next

door to the stable where he lived alone. There were cuts
on his face and one eye was badly bruised.

She lit the lamp and Amsy sat at a table, getting his
breath. She put a kettle on the fire, but he recovered
quickly and went to the sink, pumping water, washing his
face with a cloth, laughing a little.

"You can make tea," he said. "I been beat worse than this
many a time. Only I was younger."

"Something has to be done," she said.

"Like what? Complain against Rag Shade? Get him a ten
dollar fine, paid by Morg?"

"Like running those men out of town!"

"Sure," he said. "I'm for that. Tell Johnny he's got to make
sure of the vote. Then we'll run 'em out of town. But without J. Bracket we can't come close."

"Yes," she said. "I can see that."

"Never did see Morg so riled," said Amsy. "The way they
came in and all. Something's gone wrong for him. You know,
maybe we got a chance, at that."

She sat at the table. "No. We haven't really got a chance,
not this election. Maybe next year. We can try and we can
build. That's the democratic way."

"If Johnny can vote his Mex friends, we got a chance."

"He might be able to force the issue. But will he?"

Amsy shot her a quick look. "Well, now, that's another
matter. I don't know if he will. You oughta have an idea."

She left soon after and he went to a wall mirror and
looked at his reflection. He had been unwilling to allow her
to see the humiliation, the grief and rage which were in
him. It would have been dangerous to offer even token
resistance, he told himself, the others would have joined
Shade in beating him. If he were only younger . . .

No use, he told himself. Younger, there would have been
a killing. Someone would have died. Better a man should
steady down, accept the fact that he can't fight with his
hands and feet, begin using his head. Morg Field was the
target. Rag Shade and the others were nothing without their
boss.

Yet he knew full well that even with the Armindez faction
voting there would be no electoral victory over Field. Ballots could be stolen, ballots could be mis-counted. So long
as he held the power of money and guns, Morg Field would
rule the town and the county. He used the warm water to

soak away dirt from the cuts on his face. It was a bitter
night for Amsy Buchanan, one-time Indian fighter and Army
Scout.

Susan Carter sat at the corner table in The Four Aces
and listened to Tom Mulloy make his report. Nobody cared
whether she listened.

Morg didn't even realize she was taking laudanum. She
had been careful this time, it was true, but he knew all the
symptoms and if he had been paying attention he would
have realized the fact. Nobody paid any attention to her
any more. She was a piece of flesh to be used when needed,
that was all.

"Armindez is the one. Get rid of him, you got it made.
None of 'em have got any guts without him," Mulloy said.
"They know Bracket's behind him. They're like kids; they
got to have a protector."

Field said, "Armindez. Yes, I've been thinking about him."

"Jarret talks to him," said Mulloy. "Jarret ain't been comin'
too clean with me, lately."

"I been thinkin' about Jarret, too."

Susan Carter wondered if they knew as much as she did.
Sitting at her window, moving about town like a ghost, un-
noticed and uncared for, had sharpened her senses. People
talked and she listened and understood. Morg sensed there
was unrest, but he still controlled the situation, she thought
hopelessly.

Mulloy said, "We could take care of Armindez."

"He's a friend of Bracket," said Field.

"I don't understand about Bracket. You put him there,
you're ready to take him out of there. Why worry?"

"I don't worry. I think," said Morg. "The boys just beat
up on Amsy. It's a start. The rest will take care of itself."

"About Armindez?"

"What about him?"

"Supposin' Bracket can't find out what happens?"

"If he couldn't, he'd be dumber than you are."

Mulloy's sallow face flushed. "I ain't all that dumb that
I don't know you're scared of Johnny."

Susan thought that Morg would explode, sitting there on
his chair. Then she realized he was too clever for ordinary
blow-ups, too well organized to allow Mulloy to upset him.

He said, "Tom, you know better than that. Please try to use your head."

Mulloy got up and jammed his hat on his head. He showed his yellow, uneven teeth. "Sure, Morg. I'll keep lookin' around and see what I can learn."

He left the saloon. Susan Carter sat very still. Morg did not even glance at her. She was beginning to realize that he hated her almost as much as she hated him.

Still without looking at her, he said, "It's about time we had a showdown."

"Yes, Morg?" She was very calm.

"You're on that stuff again."

Then he had known it, but didn't care. She said, "Anything you say."

"We've been through for some time."

"Have we?"

"I'm goin' to give you a break, Susan. You don't deserve it, but I'm goin' to give it to you."

"Thanks."

He ignored her irony. "After elections, I'm going to let you open up down below the tracks. A topflight house. If you want to go to Denver or Frisco and pick out some girls, that's fine with me. You'll run it, own it so far as anybody knows. We split it fifty-fifty."

"A . . . house?" She had expected anything but this. He might have sent her away. He might have had her killed.

"That's where you came from, ain't it? What's wrong with a good, clean house?"

She sipped the wine in the slender glass. "Why, nothing. I've been in nasty, dirty houses, like you say."

"Then don't argue with me. I got troubles enough."

"I'm not arguing. I'm just wondering."

"Nothin' to wonder about. Field City is growin'. It'll grow some more when this panic's over. You'll do fine in a place down there."

"Below the tracks."

He looked at her in amazement. "You don't think you could open a joint above the tracks?"

"Why, no," she said. "Of course not." She had to be very careful. "Next month, after you're elected?"

"That's right. Got to be careful."

"Oh, yes. You do have to be careful."

"Well," he said, "that's settled, then. We'll drink to it."

The bartender brought more wine and a whiskey for Morg. She sat there, trying to smile. Morg was actually genial for the first time in weeks. He toasted her, had another drink. She knew where this would lead—upstairs to her bedroom. She was frozen and scorched alternately, watching him exchange greetings with the townsfolk who came and went in the bar. An hour passed and she had not uttered a word.

Tom Mulloy came in about midnight. He was flushed and excited. He sat down without removing his hat.

"The hat, Tom," said Morg Field. "Manners, remember."

Mulloy put both hands on the table. He said in a hoarse whisper, "Lonely Jones just made Crabtree open the Assay Office. He registered some claims on Picayune Creek."

All effects of alcohol left Field in an instant. "He bring in any color?"

"Plenty. Crabtree showed me."

"The old joker really found something?"

"Monty and Bracket went to the telegraph office and sent wires for equipment."

"They register claims, too?"

"You know they did. Comin' in here at night, tryin' to keep it quiet. Good thing we got our men in the right spot, Morg. This could be big."

"Yeah," said Field. "This could be very big. A gold rush. Money comin' out of everybody's ears. Prices goin' sky-high. And me with the only bank in town."

Susan Carter said, "And that house below the tracks. A gold rush crowd could make it profitable."

"Right," said Morg. "Glad you think that way. We'll open before elections if it pays off."

"But how about the gold?" demanded Mulloy. "How about gettin' some of it?"

"I'll take mine right here," said Field. "I won't be needin' to wash gold, except when it comes over the counter."

Mulloy got up. "I don't own a bank, Morg. I'm headin' for Picayune Creek."

"Deputize Moriarty," said Field carelessly. "It'll be a big thing. Field City will be on every map."

"And I'll be the biggest madame in the West," said Susan Carter. "How wonderful."

Again he did not notice her tone. He was already leaving to check with Crabtree at the Assay Office. She sat with her glass of wine for a moment, then went slowly up the stairs.

The blue bottle would get her through the initial shock. She could drift away on opium clouds for that night.

Tomorrow was another day. Before the drug took hold she could plan. Now that she knew the future laid out for her by Morg Field she could try to get out of the trap. For a moment she had a terrible premonition. She could see herself laid out, cold and dead, with no mourners. A pine box and a hole on Boot Hill would be her ending, she thought.

And Morgan Field would go on, ruling and killing and destroying lives that he might wallow in wealth.

She increased the dose of laudanum in the wineglass.

## chapter ten

LONELY JONES SAID, "There's somethin' about pickin' it up, diggin' it or pannin' it out of water, nothin' but your own elbow grease, nobody to tell you what or when. It gets 'em. The fever, that's part of it, but mainly it's somethin' for nothin' that they can't resist."

Men were coming up toward Picayune Creek like sluggard ants, bearing the paraphernalia of placer mining, horseback, afoot, in wagons, every way. Johnny stood against the base of Lost Peak, a hunk of rock thrust like a fist against the sky. Monty was happily working the pan at the edge of their staked claim.

Lonely said, "Every train'll bring more of 'em. In a week wagon parties will be wheelin' in. The telegram did it. The news will reach to Texas, to California."

Johnny said, "I didn't realize it would stir people up that much."

"Gold," said Lonely. "It's been a word to stir men since ancient Egypt."

They had staked their claims near to Lost Peak, upstream from the plateau. Tom Mulloy rode around the rock and reined in. He was leading a pack pony.

"Welcome," said Lonely. "You're the first."

But Mulloy was not amused, Johnny saw at once. The false geniality which he had worn like a loose mask was gone. His eyes were yellowish, his mouth grim below the straggly moustache. He got down from the horse and stalked to where Monty was washing a residue from the small flume.

"Keepin' it to yourselves, were you?" he snarled like an animal.

Up the hill, toiling, sweating, came a figure laden with more than he was able to carry with any degree of ease. It was young Randy Holt and Johnny felt a twinge of remorse. To take the youngster away from his safe, if onerous job, on a fake discovery of gold was to assume responsibility he wished he could avoid. Still, it was part of the overall game. He watched carefully as Mulloy strode to the little rock cairns marked with names of the owner for whom they had filed claims.

"Took care of yourn," Mulloy went on. He had not yet seen young Holt. "Lonely, Monty, Bracket, Mary Jones . . ."

Young Holt managed to tote his burden to the corner marking of Mary's holding. He slipped down there, resting his pack. He managed to gasp, "I put my name here, on this claim. Mr. Bracket, you're my witness."

Mulloy stopped, surveyed Holt as though looking down at a bug. Then he kicked the youth in the ribs and said, "Get outa here. I already got this located."

"Mr. Bracket . . ." Then Holt gathered himself. He got slowly to his feet. He spread his legs to maintain balance and spoke directly to Mulloy.

"You hadn't set foot on this claim, Tom, and you know it. I spoke first."

"Get off it," said Mulloy. He made a pushing motion at Randy, which the boy avoided.

Then Johnny saw the old, half-rusted gun hanging at Holt's belt. Mulloy spotted it at the same time, stepped two paces away.

Mulloy said, "Off my land or I'll kill you where you stand."

Monty was on his knees at the stream, his mouth half open. Lonely was caught flat-footed, aghast, realizing as did Johnny that Mulloy might well shoot down the armed youth and get away with it on grounds of self defense.

Johnny made his decision very swiftly. He had already been in motion. Now he leaped between Mulloy and his target.

"Holt's right. He was on the claim before you were."

"You want a hand? You can get it," said Mulloy. His voice

rose. "You been lordin' it around long enough with your fast draw. Try me, Bracket. Go ahead, try me."

He actually assumed the gunslinger's crouch. Johnny had not seen the gesture since El Paso, he was nearly bemused by it, the clawing hand near the gun butt, the sidewinder jutting of the jaw, the sideways move to present a lesser vulnerability. Just in time, he moved even closer to Mulloy.

"There's plenty of space below there. Don't be a damn fool, Marshal."

"I say this is mine and I'll defend it."

"I say you're a sucker," said Johnny.

Then he dropped his left shoulder, feinted and threw his right fist in a short arc. Mulloy's hand was dropping to his gun. Johnny's punch beat him clearly by a half second. Mulloy's head spun sideways on his shoulders, then Johnny hit him in the belly, so that he doubled up and turned and fell on his face.

Lonely, his poise recovered, had Mulloy's gun in a jiffy. Johnny rubbed his knuckles.

Randy Holt said in a shaky voice, "I suppose he'll try to kill me, now."

"That's what he was up to," Johnny said. He looked at Lonely. "You sure knew your book. Gold—gold makes people do crazy things."

Mulloy was on his knees. He growled, "I'll show you all. The sun'll never set on you, none of you."

People were coming up the hill. Johnny went to where Mulloy was regaining his feet. He took hold of the Marshal's shoulder and shook him once.

"You're the law in town, no place else. You make one bad move in this camp and you'll hang. You know miner's law? Let me tell you, one sample and you won't live to learn more about it. Now get down there and stake your claim next to Holt's, or get out of here and don't come back. Because, Tom . . . you're no gunfighter. You may be a killer, but man, you're slow, plumb slow."

He turned Mulloy and urged him downhill, walking him off the area which might be rightfully claimed by Randy Holt. After a few steps, Mulloy began to tremble. His mouth worked, he clawed at his moustache. There was a lump on his jaw and his middle ached.

He said, finally, "You shouldn't've done it, Johnny. You should've gunned me."

"You don't mean that. You wouldn't rather be dead."

Mulloy bent and dashed water from the creek on his face. He knelt a moment, then looked up.

"Gold. That's the answer. Runnin' cattle is too slow. I been around too long to wait. Morg's got it, all of it. I want somethin' quick."

"Help yourself," said Johnny. "There's plenty agree with you. They'll be here within the hour. Set your claim." He had no compunction about this footless, dangerous man. "But don't fool with young Holt, nor with any of us."

"When I come at you, I won't be foolin'," Mulloy said.

"You better get Rag Shade to help you," said Johnny. "You and him, you talk a lot alike."

He turned his back and returned to help Randy Holt arrange his corner markers. Lonely worked with him in silence while Holt explained how he had quit his job and got ahead of all the others and toiled up the hill. If Johnny and Monty and Lonely were in on it, he knew he could make it, and then he would be free of Morg Field. His mother had objected but this time he wouldn't be deterred. She had prevailed on him not to leave and go to another town, but this wasn't so far from home, he didn't feel like he was deserting her, just up at Lost Peak, on the Picayune.

Johnny said, "Sure Randy. Look, take off that gun, will you?"

The youngster flushed. "I thought I ought to have one. It was in the attic. Guess I was wrong."

"It could get you killed," said Johnny. "Take it off and we'll see nobody bothers you."

Back against Lost Peak, watching the eager caravan making its way to the creek, Lonely said, "I salted that claim pretty good. He'll wash out a couple hundred."

"That ain't the point, is it, Lonely?"

"Well . . . no."

They could see the vanguard of the hopefuls. Several local citizens of dubious character; little Sanders, a handyman, Sticky from the livery stable. These did not matter, they had little else to do. The Swede showed, representing himself and Moriarty, then the out of towners began to get to the creek.

There were old-timers who yelled at Lonely, there were youngsters who knew little more than Randy Holt, there was a couple, the woman as sunburned and boot-tough as her mate, there were strong men and weak ones and they all had the same idea: Gold is where you find it, take it and look for more.

Lonely said, "If they wasn't here they'd be on some other wild goose chase."

"Sure, I know," said Johnny. But he didn't like it. He couldn't reconcile himself to deluding all these people. He turned and went slowly around Lost Peak into the canyon which dead-ended a mile away against the rising range of the Padres. He heard Monty call Lonely to examine for color and kept walking. It was a desolate, stony arroyo where the cattle never drifted despite the nearness to water. He stumbled, kicking a loose rock with soft boot, scowling at the pain in his foot.

Then he sat down, tilting his hat brim against the sun. He picked up the loose stone, turned it over. It gleamed dully where it was not covered with dirt. He had been too long in western country not to know what that sheen could mean.

He looked hastily around. No one was in view. For the first time in his life he knew the meaning of the fever he had been speculating upon for the past hours. He had been able to scorn it, knowing that the stream had been salted, that it was all a fake. Now his breath came short, he was dry and wet, hot and cold, all in the same moment. He wanted to call Lonely, but the thought of the others, the ones they had summoned with their false alarm, deterred him as he knew a strange fear.

He managed to walk, weak-kneed, to the base of Lost Peak. There was a small, rough growth of sage. He found himself on his knees, concealing the small boulder, no bigger than his two fists.

He got up, brushing his trousers, trying hard to control the shakiness he felt to his core. He moistened his lips with the end of his tongue. He adjusted his hat brim with a sweep of both palms.

He walked around Lost Peak. He could see the miners, stringing out along the creek, calling to one another, making a charivari of it. The weather was as fine as it could get in springtime in the Territory.

He finally got Lonely Jones to one side. He had to take hold of the prospector and drag him out of sight to the place where he had deposited his discovery.

After a moment, Lonely said, "It ain't possible."

"You mean it's gold? That's a nugget?"

"I walked past this arroyo a thousand times," Lonely said, stunned. "I worked Picayune Creek. I been over this part of the country with a fine tooth comb. And I never thought to walk into Lost Canyon."

"I didn't even know it had a name."

"Who'd bother to call it anything? It's no place. It's a place nobody ever wanted to be, not even rattlers." Then Lonely shook himself. "Now, this'll be easy. Everybody's out there, pannin' for dust. Just leave 'em be. Get a good horse. Go to Territorial City and register the claims. I'll get my compass and figure it out. You go on, keep people away from here."

Johnny said, "What about my—our nugget?"

"Take it with you," said Lonely. "You know what? Even if there was gold in the Picayune, it wouldn't come close to measurin' up to what we'll take out of here."

Johnny started away, then paused. He said, "Hey, one little thing."

"What's that?"

"I'm filin' a claim part in the name of that boy, Randy Holt."

"That's your business," said Lonely. "You're the one that found it."

He went back to surveying the land in his mind, pacing off from Lost Peak. Johnny went shakily around to where the newcomers were unlimbering equipment preparatory to washing the bed of Picayune. He caught up his horse, told Monty he was going on business and rode down foward the ranch.

He saw Banning in the west pasture and gave instructions to keep the stock grazed and to hire a cook if necessary. He rode down to the house and for a moment sat alone in the comfortable parlor which Monty, against all precedent in the county—or in the entire West—had created out of low chairs and a couch lined with cushions.

Riches, he thought. His mind was weary. He had not bargained for riches.

This house, this room, had been created by thought and doing, by careful handiwork, out of life. What would be the effect of riches? Certainly the value of this room would vanish. He would be able to build a mansion to make the ranch house look like a shabby cabin. Yet it was not a shabby cabin, it was a place created with intent to please, a place to live in, a place to die in.

It was a moment of illumination, of startling white clarity. He could look at his hands, calloused and hard and think that he need no longer abuse them with hard ranch work and in the same instant know that he was completely ignorant of what it would mean not to use them for daily existence. He was afraid, he was confused.

The moment passed. Wealth was something which could buy comfort and easy living for Mary. Lonely would never have to roam the desert in hot summer. Monty could go back to England for a visit any time he liked. Young Randy could make his mother proud.

The people who had come from far and wide could share in the discovery if the vein held out. There would be heavy machinery, laborers hired to bring prosperity to the town. Morgan Field would not be the only wealthy man in the county, the balance would shift. It would bring a new day for the county all the way around.

He got up and went briskly to the corral. It was a long ride to Territorial City.

## chapter eleven

THE STREET WAS lighted bright as day, although it was past the supper hour. The Four Aces reeked with unwashed men, the new, two storied place called the Elephant's Ear, owned and operated by Madame Victoria of ill fame, gave off the raucous sound of revelry. Morg Field exchanged a word with Moriarty, then paused before the bank to ponder the intricacies of the situation.

Tomorrow was the day the mortgage on Johnny Bracket's ranch was due. The following week was Election Day. Money was rolling in from all directions. Yet he felt that he was losing his grip upon the town.

There were too many new people, none to be trusted. They respected him, certainly, but they owed him nothing. They would vote for him because he had passed the word that he would keep the town wide open. The question was, did he want to remain in the sort of place Field City had become, a volcano which could burst forth at any moment, enveloping all in the fire of violence and destruction?

Mary Jones hurried by. He stepped back to avoid being seen by her, anger shaking him to his heels. He knew then that he could not depart from Field City without accomplishing certain aims. Darkness drew a screen before him as he turned and groped his way into the back room of his bank.

Shade joined him before he had finished his first drink, then Susan Carter came in, wearing a long, dark cloak over a tight fitted black dress.

Shade said, "Never did see a bigger ruckus. Beats me, the way things changed overnight."

"Gold will bring in the thieves," said Field.

"So long as we get our share," said Shade.

"We're getting it." He looked at Susan. "It's almost time to open that house. Madame Victoria will help get it started."

"A great woman, the Madame," said Susan, managing a tight smile.

"She knows her business." Field turned as there was a knock at the door. "That'll be Mulloy."

Shade admitted the Marshal. His face was drawn, his skin ochre colored, his eyes were sunken. He reached for the whiskey bottle and poured himself a slug which he swallowed, gulping.

Field said, "Finally got through to you, did it?"

"Two hundred and four dollars," said Mulloy. "That's what I took out. For all that sweat, two hundred and four dollars."

"They worked it very neat," said Field. "They salted the creek, knowin' all the time the strike was up the canyon. They foresaw a rush, brought it in, steered it wrong for a while 'til they registered all the claims they could. They put Amsy and Armindez and all their friends in it. You could have filed, Tom."

"I thought I could clean up in Picayune Creek."

"You didn't ask me," Field reminded him. "The minute you get loose from my apron strings you make mistakes."

"I'll have their hearts for it," said Mulloy.

"Not on your own," Field said.

"No." Mulloy sighed, drank again. "I admit it, Morg. I need you. I ain't about to try it on my own."

Shade laughed disagreeably and Susan Carter looked

away from them, at the wall. Field did not alter expression, reaching into a drawer, taking out a badge, shoving it across to Mulloy.

"You got Moriarty, the Swede and Cannon. Try and keep some kind of order. Don't close anybody down. But make them know we're still runnin' the town."

Mulloy pinned the badge to his vest. "What about Bracket?"

"I got a notion." Field leaned back and put his boots on the desk. "He won't be later than opening time tomorrow with the mortgage money."

"How do you know he's got it? They haven't been able to get out any ore, not yet."

"He was up at the capital," said Field. "They formed a company, Territorial Mining. What the hell, I'd have done the same. The bankers gave him all the money he needed."

"So. He's got the money, he's got the ranch, he's got the mine. And he took the girl."

Morg Field said softly, "You been outa touch, Tom. You been up there pannin' for gold. You don't know what's goin' on."

"I know that Texan's gettin' away with murder."

Rag Shade laughed. Mulloy looked at him, then at Morg Field, who was smiling in a bleak manner.

"Okay, what's my part?"

"You're goin' back on the job. You're goin' to walk Main Street, wearin' that badge. You don't hear anything out of order, you don't see anything but maybe a drunk actin' up a little. You check out Madame Victoria's, but don't get your nose in too deep."

"Can't I do anything to Bracket?"

"Not unless he gets out of line," said Morg. "If he does, you can throw him in jail. Moriarty, the Swede and Cannon will be there to help."

Mulloy said, "I don't need 'em."

"Sure, Tom. But they'll be around."

"I sure would like to be in on it." Mulloy hesitated. "You're not sore because I went minin', are you, Morg? I figured we could use a quick dollar."

"You figured *you* could use it," Morg corrected him. "But we've been together a long time, Tom. Forget it."

They shook hands. Mulloy went out the rear door. His

shoulders were slightly stooped with hard work and disappointment.

Morg said, "He won't be any good to me for very long, now. Do it up right, Shade. You're next in line."

The foreman laughed. "Here today gone tomorrow, huh, Morg? It's all in a lifetime." He followed Mulloy into outer darkness.

Susan Carter asked, "How can you be certain they can handle Bracket?"

"I'm not."

"But you do have to take the chance?"

He tilted his chair and put his hands behind his head, relaxing. "There's the election. Nobody can tell about these newcomers. Gold rushes don't last forever, pretty soon they start heavy mining and we get another breed, the dummies that work for wages. I don't know if I'm goin' to like that kind of town. I got to be ready to jump whichever way is best. Bracket can get in my way."

"He's already got your girl."

Morg Field said, "You have a nasty way of repeating that." He took his feet down deliberately, leaned forward and suddenly slapped her across the face. She fell from the chair and rolled on the floor.

He puffed on the cigar, sitting there, a small red spot on each cheek, brooding over her. She pulled herself erect, her head spinning. She got the door open and left.

He sat back. His teeth cut through the end of the cigar. He threw it from his mouth, took another from a box on his desk and lit it, forcing himself to pull smoothly and evenly upon it.

Johnny Bracket was soaking himself free of soil and sweat in Simon Jarret's bath. Clean clothing was folded nearby. Atop the pile was a money belt and a cocked revolver. In the belt was over eight thousand dollars, enough to pay off the mortgage and interest due the bank and to buy equipment needed at the mine.

The door opened and Moriarty stuck in his head. "That you, Johnny? Everything okay?"

"Just dandy. Shut the door, you're creatin' a draft." Moriarty complied, withdrawing from view. He had no use for the coarse Irish deputy. He was irritated with the way things were going in town.

Mary no longer dared walk the streets. They were coming in from all over the country—from all over the world—the scum, the harpies, the vultures who hung around the edges of gold diggings to pick up the leavings. Amsy Buchanan was up at the Picayune and the stable was being run by a Negro boy and next to the stable was the house and saloon operated by Madame Victoria. Morg Field had done nothing to tame things down.

Now that Mulloy was back there would be no change, Johnny knew. Mulloy had been bad enough a year ago, now he was a viciously disposed failure. He had thought to corner the placer mining while others shifted to the diggings. He had let it be known in loud accents that he believed he had been double-crossed.

Which, in a way, he had. He had fallen for Lonely's chicanery in salting the creek and had steadfastly held in his belief.

It was an uneasy situation. Johnny felt some guilt, but on the other hand, he thought that when it was all over the town would settle down and then it would be indeed a metropolis, buzzing with both mining and cattle interests. Morg couldn't control it, then. There would be too many to see through him. Lonely had laid it all out to him and Monty had agreed.

Still, Johnny had liked the old, quiet town, enjoyed such citizens as Armindez—now a prosperous mine owner-to-be —and the decency and quietude of the neatly laid out and well kept streets. The caterwauling of the multitude was a desecration to the town founded by Mary's father.

He was not unaware of his influence over the oldtimers of the community. When Sime Jarret came in and leaned against the door he stepped from the cooling water and dried himself on a large, coarse towel.

"I'll be right out. I know you've got customers waiting," he said.

"Yep. Business is fine. That Italian barber I hired is makin' me rich. Better'n gold minin' for a fella like me," said Jarret. "What I wanted to talk about, Johnny, I ain't so sure about the election."

"Sure about what?"

Jarret twisted his hands. "About bein' Mayor if I should get elected. Things is different, nowadays."

"You mean the job scares you?"

"Well . . . not to give you a short answer . . . yes."

Johnny reached for his shirt. Then he remembered the money belt he had reluctantly bought at Lonely's suggestion, and buckled its unpleasant clamminess about his narrow waist. "You'll have help. You can appoint people to a Council or somethin', get rid of Mulloy and Moriarty and them."

"What if they don't want to be fired? I'm no fighter, Johnny, you know that. Miss Mary talked me into makin' a run for it, on account of the way Morg does everything. But I'm no good at them things."

"You're the only candidate. And you haven't been elected, not yet. I think you will be elected, because we're going to police the polls. But maybe Morg can beat us, some way or another."

"I just can't help hopin' he will win," said Jarret unhappily.

He went back into his shop as voices called his name. Johnny finished dressing. It was a lousy deal, he thought, anyway you looked at it. He shrugged on a light jacket and went out into the barber shop. Several people called his name and he spoke briefly to them. He went onto the street and started toward the Jones house, then remembered that his horse, at the livery stable, might have been neglected and decided to make sure it was fed.

He saw Moriarty and the Swede and Cannon, then he saw Mulloy wearing his badge. They were sauntering along Main Street paying no attention to brawling, howling drunks who came out of The Four Aces and other joints which had opened up like sores along the way. He shook his head and turned past the hotel into the stable yard.

There was no light in the barn, which was odd. He fumbled for the lantern, which always hung on a peg just inside the door.

He heard a small sound and whirled. There was light from the new place, Madame Victoria's, just across the lot from the stable. In a moment of whirling action, when someone grabbed his arms from behind, he caught a glimpse of a face. Then he was slugged alongside the head.

He continued to fight them. They held tight and again someone hit him. This time it was a stunning blow which drove him face downward to the floor. He could smell the

manure and the straw and splintered heavy timbers hurt his
cheek as they kicked him.

Not a word was spoken. He did not attempt to cry out
because he knew he would be killed if they thought he recognized them, also if they thought they might be caught in the
act, or in leaving. He was not certain they did not mean to
kill him anyway, because they rolled him over and tore at
his clothes and snatched the money belt from him and then
they kicked him some more, until he could not hold onto
consciousness, all the pain melting, everything slipping and
sailing away with the big, shattering knowledge running
through his head that he was finished and that it was a bad
end, a disgraceful end.

Then he heard a shot. He thought they had emptied it
into him, making doubly sure, but with a last flicker before
he went completely out, he knew they would not fire a gun
because it might attract attention, which they did not want.

He did not even know how long it was before he became
conscious and knew he was on his feet, draped against a
person who was aiding him up a flight of stairs. It had been a
slow process up to then, he realized, because they had only
made a couple of the treads, which were, oddly, thickly
carpeted. He thrust himself against the wall and the person lifted with some small strength and he went on up toward a hall lit only by a dim, red lamp.

He knew at once he was being helped by a woman and
then he knew it was, by the perfume, Susan Carter. When
they got to the head of the stairway and he fell on his knees
she knelt beside him, panting in broken gasps.

"Johnny. You've got to make it. Crawl, anything. Someone will be coming any minute. Straight ahead. Crawl. I
can't carry you or drag you or anything any more. Crawl!"

He moved a hand, then a knee. He collapsed, but kept
worming his way along the carpet. There was, miraculously,
a door, which she opened, falling through with him, lying
alongside him, her breath mingling with his. She had been
drinking and there was another, acrid odor which he dimly
recognized. He had known a whore in El Paso who had
been on the laudanum and had killed herself because of it
and other matters.

She said, "I don't know if this'll work. I don't know. Do
you know where you are?"

"Madame Victoria's?"

"Yes. It was the nearest. And the only place you might hide until you can fight them."

"Mary Jones's house," he managed to whisper.

"No. They'd have killed you if I didn't scare them off." She pressed a small revolver into his hand. "They were going to kill you."

"Rag Shade," he said. "Halliday. Frey."

"You couldn't prove it."

He couldn't think very well. "You saw them."

"Johnny, make some sense. I couldn't testify."

Of course she couldn't. She could get killed for doing this much. "Okay," he said. "You do what's best."

He closed his eyes. The effort of getting into this whore's bedroom had been too much. He went to sleep again.

She looked at him in the dim light of a tiny lamp. Then she got up. Madame fixed up a nice room, at that. There was a clean bed. A basin of water, towels which had not yet turned tattle-tale gray. Better than the last crib Susan had occupied, where Morg had found her in 'Frisco.

She pushed back the fuzziness of mind which laudanum had inflicted and through which she had managed to act by a tremendous effort of will. She was proud of herself but the action had just begun, she knew. There was still Madame Victoria.

Firing the revolver at them had been a good thought. They had vanished without checking as to who might be after them. Now they would make themselves scarce about town until Morg learned who had to be killed next. It was necessary to cover up and to do it secretly and swiftly.

She went to the door. There was no lock on it, of course, there never was in a well conducted house. She eased it open and slipped into the hall. The lamp with the red shade cast a weird light.

There were stumbling footsteps on the rear stairs. She flattened herself against the wall. A tall man in the black coat of the tinhorn whispered, "Mona? That you?"

"Mona's in the parlor," she answered. "Better not let the Madame catch you."

"The hell with her," he said. He was drunk enough to cause trouble.

"You know what'll happen if you're caught coming in this way. Why don't you go in the front and send Mona up here? I'll help you."

"You hate the Madame, too, eh?" He chuckled. "Everybody hates the goddam Madame."

He went back down the stairs, staggering a bit. Susan Carter remained against the wall, thinking hard. If Mona was foolish enough to try to meet her gambler lover, then it was best to remain here and wait. It was agonizing to have to be silent and immobile, every nerve in her screamed for release. She bit at her lip until it bled. Her nails crushed into the dry palms of her hands. She wanted a touch of the drug as she had never yearned for it.

Hate, she thought, was a good crutch. She thought hard about Morgan Field, of the long list of crimes he had committed against her, not the least of which was that of making her love him for a time. Far better to have remained in 'Frisco—she would have died before now and been out of it.

She was trembling when the woman came up the front stairs of the rambling establishment, a blonde with weak features, scared in the half-light and startled to find Susan Carter waiting.

"Which room do you use to meet your man?" Susan asked.

"Uh—that one," said Mona, pointing.

"All right. Go down and tell Madame I want to see her, right now, in the end room, near the stairs. Then you'll be free to do what you want."

"I don't understand," faltered the blonde woman.

She summoned force to dominate the wavering creature. "Do as I say! And hurry!"

The waiting was unendurable. Her skin itched, she was wet with perspiration. She went back into the room, leaving the door ajar. Johnny was still unconscious. She wondered how seriously he was hurt, if she had made a big mistake.

She might have made it to the Jones house, she thought. Even if she had only carried him out on Main Street there might have been friends to help him, perhaps the Mexicans. But she had been watching Johnny for months and she needed him. It was her only chance.

There was a sound and she whirled and faced Madame Victoria. She said, "Oh! I need help, Madame."

The woman was tall and birdlike. She wore greying hair in a pompadour. She was dressed in black bombazine and resembled nothing more than a school teacher. Her nose was hooked, her lips a hard, thin line.

"You're Morgan Field's woman. What are you doing here with a drunk?"

"He's not drunk."

The woman went close and moved the lamp so that light fell across Johnny's bruised features. "I see. Johnny Bracket."

"Yes. He needs a doctor."

"Did Morg Field's men do this to him?"

"Yes. Please don't argue. I'll pay. I need your doctor."

"I don't argue, woman. Nor do I buy a pig in a poke. What's the deal?"

"I want to hide him here until he recovers. I want to buy time, you can sell it to me."

The woman folded her arms and stared into space. "Morg Field runs the town. Why should I go against him?"

"For money. And because you pay him too much for protection."

"You know that?" Madame Victoria nodded. "You know a lot, I expect."

"I know all about Morg." She hesitated, then went on, "Did you know he is planning to open a new, big house?"

"No. He promised not to."

"I'll give you a hundred dollars now, more later," said Susan. Her nerves were beginning to go.

Johnny coughed and blood trickled from his mouth.

Madame Victoria said, "Let's put him on the bed. They must have booted him. He does need a doctor, all right."

"They meant to kill him," said Susan.

"Certainly they did. Men don't play games in this country, you ought to know that. Bracket's got too many underdogs on his side to make a fight against Field. I don't want any part of this, truth to tell."

Susan lifted her skirt and took money from her stocking. "Two hundred dollars."

"What if Field finds out?"

"What difference? He's going to open his own house, I tell you. If Bracket lives, you've got a chance. If he dies, none of us has got a chance."

The beady eyes narrowed. "If he dies I suppose we could dump the body."

"In Deep Canyon," said Susan with certain irony. "A lead pipe cinch."

Madame Victoria took the money. "I guess we can trust

Doc. For a consideration. Happens he's here, checking on the girls. But I suppose you knew that."

"I knew it, but I didn't plan it," said Susan. "If you don't hurry he may die right now."

"You'll back me if he lives and beats out Field?"

"It's everything I'm planning for," said Susan. "It's why I scared off Shade and the others, it's why we're here. Can't you see?"

"Oh, I can see. I can also see that this could cost me my business. And more. There's nothing worse than having the boss of a town against you." She fingered the money. "You can get more later?"

"Yes. Plenty more."

"It's a long chance and I shouldn't be taking it." She went to the door and into the hall. Susan followed her.

There were noises in the room Mona had indicated. Madame Victoria made a face. She said in disgust, "Love! A washed out blonde and a skinny gambler. I'd throw them out in a minute, excepting girls are scarce." She slapped the bills against her skinny thigh. "And I might need a man beholden to me around with a gun." She looked sharply at Susan. "Look, I can't handle the trade, way things are. You wouldn't like to help out on the side?"

"I couldn't manage it," said Susan.

"I suppose not, with Field snooping all the time. Well, any time you could, you are welcome."

"I'll have to go, now. Morg'll be expecting me."

"Go ahead." Madame Victoria straightened her narrow shoulders. "Go on. When I make a bargain, I keep it."

Susan left the place the way she had entered. It was dark as pitch in the space between the livery stable and the street. She went around in back of the hotel and came out into the light sauntering and outwardly composed. She made herself walk slowly to The Four Aces and assumed her place in the far corner. It was not easy but she managed to appear calm.

When Morg Field came in she was sipping wine. The effects of that morning's laudanum had begun to wear off. She felt dried out and shaky. She could not resort to the blue bottle now, however, nor at any time until it was all over, one way or the other.

She was able to sit quietly while Rag Shade came in and made his report by whispering in Morg's ear and she could see the alteration of Morg's color, the way he responded with anger and fear, a satisfying thing to her.

"You mean he got away?"

"Someone took a shot at us, I tell you."

"Then that someone saw you."

Shade was silent. He was also sullen. He was fully aware, as was Field, that the slip had finally been made, that the fat was in the fire.

"You sure you didn't finish him?"

"He should be dead. But he ain't where we left him. I snuck back to check."

"If he lives and if someone saw you . . ." Field broke off, staring at Susan. "You better go upstairs."

She rose obediently, smiled at them. "Good night, gentle-men. Pleasant dreams."

It was a chance, she thought. They were worried. If things worked out, she might yet be free. The steps did not seem nearly so steep tonight.

# chapter twelve

WHEN JOHNNY AWAKENED the first time he was under the influence of an opiate administered by the Doc. He dimly saw and comprehended that a woman was sitting beside the bed and supposed he was in the hospital.

"Mary?" he asked tentatively.

"Not so's you'd notice it," said Madame Victoria.

"Can't . . . seem . . . to place you."

"Don't bother. You got a cracked rib and various and sundry bad concussions. Keep quiet."

"The mortgage money. They got the payment."

"And Morg Field's got your ranch. If you don't get well and be ready for a fight we're all in a picklement."

"Fight?" He drowsed despite all effort. "They beat hell outa me, lady."

"I'm no lady and you still got a lot of hell in you," said Madame Victoria. She added as he went back to sleep, "I hope. If you ain't, then I sure as hell am backin' the wrong entry."

The second time he came wider awake. Susan Carter had taken the place of the tall woman. He stared at her, then around at the room.

"I remember. It's Madame Victoria's house."

"You're bad hurt," she said rapidly. "You had us all scared."

"Mary? Did anybody tell Mary?"

"I got word to her that you were hurt and hiding. She went up to the diggings, to her grandfather."

"The ranch?"

"Morg took it over."

"Hell of a thing. Laid up in a whorehouse."

"You can get well, Doc says so. They won't find you here. Listen to me, will you, Johnny?"

"I can get up from here." He tried but blackness spun around him, decorated with stars all in a row.

"Morg made a bad move, do you see? You had him scared and mad and he put Shade on you and robbed you. But they didn't kill you."

"You fired the shot, or they would've made it."

She said, "I want out, Johnny. I want all the way out. That's all I'll ever ask of anyone."

His weakness engulfed him, made her words meaningless. He tried to find something to hang onto, which would keep him conscious, thought of Mary again, swallowed hard.

Then he looked at the dark woman. "A man only thinks about himself when he's hurt. Thing is, what about you? I mean, besides you want out and all."

She stared back at him, her face in the light of the dim lamp naked, helpless.

"What about me? Nothing about me. I'm a whore."

"I wouldn't say that."

"You don't have to."

He struggled again with his slippery intelligence.

"Why are you here, with me?"

"A whore has her pride. She loses it in the end, of course, because that is the way of life. Meantime, there is this wish to be a person, to demonstrate against the world."

"Morg did something bad to you, huh?"

"Morg is evil."

"I didn't think so, at first. A man on the make, I thought. No better, no worse than any other."

"I loved him once."

There was silence in the small room.

She arose. "I have to show myself. It's not easy to get in and out of here."

"Could you send a telegram?"

"Why, yes. I guess so. But it will be reported to Morg."

"Yes, of course it would. That would be dangerous."

She said, "If Madame Victoria sent it, maybe you could get away with it."

He said, "I'll talk to her." He closed his eyes. He should think about Susan Carter, he should try to understand what she was doing and why, but his head hurt. When she left the room he lay there trying to put back the pain and organize a plan but it was very difficult.

Mary, he thought, would be frantic. And Lonely would be thinking and wondering. Banning would have reported the loss of the ranch to Lonely. Trouble would be brewing and Monty would be crushed. Monty had put everything he had into the ranch.

Of course they had the mining property, but it was not the same. Further, if Morg Field continued to grow there would be no guarantee that they could hold the mines against his power. The town had become unsafe for anyone siding Johnny Bracket.

The door opened and Madame Victoria came in. She stared down at him imperturbable.

"What's this about a telegram, Bracket?"

"It's to my father, in Texas."

"You have a father?"

"Joe Bracket."

"Where is he at?"

"Down El Paso way."

"You have two brothers?"

"Toole and Sam, but never mind them. Pa will decide about them."

"You're one of those Brackets?" Her face was flinty. "One of those Texas Brackets?"

"I'm one of 'em."

She said sharply, "Farwell was where Toole broke up my place. Sam got me in Dodge City. And now I've got you on my hands."

He raised his head. "Why don't you call Morg Field and get even?"

She took a deep breath. "I'd like nothing better. But I made a deal."

He said, "And you know what would happen if Morg found out you made it."

"You're smart, like the rest of them," she said. "What do I put in the wire?"

"Just this: Could use some help. You got any handy?"

She said, "Field's got the telegraph office covered, you know that."

"Yeah, I know. But if you sign it with your name, maybe they won't pay attention to the Bracket end of it."

"Your old man would know it was from you?"

"I've been in touch."

She thought about that for a moment. "It's a long chance. But you got something. You can't figure Morg Field himself is going to read every telegram. The others are plain dumb. If I sign it, they won't be checking close."

"That's what I figure."

She said, "You'll keep your brothers off my back when they get here?"

"If I'm alive."

"You just want the family to pick up the pieces, huh?"

"There's other people involved."

"Sure. Long as it includes me."

"Madame, you're as tough as shoe leather. Just believe that you'll be well paid and you stand a better chance with me than you do with Morg Field."

"I've been out here since the first gold rush," she said. "Started teaching school, would you believe it? No matter, when I did go, I went all the way." She sighed. "I don't like any Bracket that ever lived, but I'll send you up some grub. On the way back from the telegraph office I'll buy you a forty-five and some shells. And if you live through this, I want plenty payment."

"You'll get it."

She shook her head in doubt and left him alone with his anguished worriment about the people he had brought with him to the edge of destruction.

Monty had managed a neat, well-constructed lean-to at the diggings behind Lost Peak. Mary drank hot coffee, which failed to prevent the shivers which went through her at intervals. When the sound of horses' hooves came in the night they all went taut, peering, Lonely and Monty with their rifles ready. Banning called to them, then rode in.

He was dark with anger, dismounting, accepting a cup of the hot brew. He demanded, "Where's the boss?"

Nobody knew what to tell him.

Banning said, "They come at me with papers. They held down on me, three of them, while Morg Field handed me the papers which I read. He had got a court order to take over the ranch and where was the boss?"

"We don't know," said Lonely Jones. "You might help us find him."

"They stole the money and hurt him," said Mary, her voice shaking as the tremors ran over her again.

"They come in with guns and papers," Banning said. "Silvy and Cantero, they took off pronto. I'm a cattleman. I'm no gunslinger, like Rag Shade and them."

"We hoped you might help."

"I hired out as foreman, to run cattle. I did my job. I'm owed some wages, but never mind that." He sipped at the coffee, somber hued in the light of the fire. "Field has got men in the hills, he has got Mulloy and them others in town. Every jackleg and pimp—'scuse me, Miss—will be sidin' him. He'll be up here, too."

"We're figurin' how to fight him."

"You can figure, but you can't win. Like I say, I'm no gunfighter. If the boss was here, if he had somethin' to offer, I would go along. No boss, no job."

"You think he don't want to be here?"

"If he's alive," said Banning. "If he can walk, he should be here, or some place to give orders. It's no good in my book." He took out his tally book as though to demonstrate that by which he lived. He laid it on a rock beside the fire. "Everything is in order, there. I got no men behind me, I got no boss. I'm slopin'."

Mary cried, "Monty is his partner. I'm going to marry him. Can't you stick with us?"

Monty said, "No, the man is correct. He has no stomach for it. And we may lose."

Banning stood up, emptying his cup on the fire, listening to the small hiss of the liquid evaporating into steam. "You think I'm scared. Well, mebbeso. I been up and down and around and I been in range wars and didn't run. But this situation, it's hopeless. Without the boss, you ain't got a chance. Morg Field is in a killin' mood. I know a killer."

He went to his horse. He mounted and rode out.

Mary wept for a moment in silence. Lonely poked at the fire with a stick. Monty retreated beyond the light of the fire and crouched, brooding.

Pedro Armindez came into the firelight. He was carrying a jug of tequila. There were tear stains on his brown cheeks.

"Bad news," said Lonely in dull tones.

"The people can learn nothing," said Pedro. "The town is shut tight. My wife, she has been warned. Any move will bring about her death. Worse. They told her they would give her to Madame Victoria."

Lonely said, "Mulloy is back in charge. Mulloy is mighty bad medicine, now. He hates."

"Field is at the Jenkins place," said Pedro despairingly. "Shade, Frey and Halliday have brought in cowboys to take over. They laugh a lot, my man says, they laugh quite a lot at the ranch house."

Monty retreated further from view of the others. He had made a supreme effort to put that house to rights. There was, he felt, very little left of him, now, with Johnny's steadying influence absent. His eyes fixed on the tequila jug.

"What must we do?" Pedro begged.

"I don't know," said Lonely.

Young Randy Holt came slowly around the north side of the lean-to. His face told the story, he had already got the news. He sat opposite Mary. He reached out toward her once, then drew back his hand, looked at it, put it in his pocket.

Lonely was saying, "Morg hit us real shrewd. Robbin' Johnny of the money, puttin' him out of it, that was smart. What can we do? Kill Morg? The law says he owns the ranch. The law says he's Mayor of the town. Nobody can prove he did anything to Johnny."

"There's nothing to do," said Randy Holt. "Except get our ore into town and learn what we can about Johnny."

"That's risky."

"We can't just stay here and wait."

"He's right," said Mary, trying to control her voice. "We've got wagons. And guns. We can get into town and make sure about Johnny. Someone knows where he is. That note—the boy who brought it and ran away."

Lonely said reluctantly, "There's a heap of gold among us. Mebbe two, three wagonloads. They hit us, they'll take the gold and bury us in Deep Canyon."

"Better than just sitting here, knowing nothing!" Mary rose, wiping away the last trace of tears. "I'm going to risk it in the morning."

"We'll think on it," said Lonely. "It might be the only thing to do."

Monty's tongue was dry as dust. Pedro was going to pour tequila. Maybe he could take just one, to relieve this terrible thirst which he had not known for so long but now well remembered. He moved toward the group around the fire.

It occurred to him that it didn't matter very much now, did it? Johnny was hurt, most likely dead, there was to be no wedding, no fine life in the house he had so painstakingly rebuilt. He reached for a tin cup. Pedro poured without thinking, without looking, without knowing for whom he was dispensing the strong booze.

Rag Shade lay on the low couch that Monty had built and drank whiskey from a pint bottle. His spurs had damaged the gay blanket coverlet. Frey was cooking something in the kitchen, making a foul odor and mess. Halliday was asleep in the bedroom, his muddy boots beside him on the carpeting.

Morg Field drank out of a coffee cup, looking around the place with reddened eyes. "We got to find that lousy, rotten Bracket. If he's alive, we got to finish him."

"He's dead, by now," said Shade. "This here is some house, now, ain't it? Like a woman did it up."

Morg kicked at a low chair. This was the place that had been fitted for Mary. He could see it in every cranny and crack. All set up pretty for the bride, Bracket's bride. It was a slap in the face.

"I got a hell of an idea, boss," said Shade, staring around. "It's been done before, it's bound to work again. Use this here fancy place for a whorehouse."

Field stopped pacing and grinned. "Say, that's just what I was aimin' to do, set up a house."

"It's the right distance from the mines," said Shade, enjoying himself. "To say nothin' about the lone cowboy ridin' the ranges hereabouts."

"It may be a good idea," said Field. "If you'd have made

sure of Bracket we could count on it." Use of Mary's house as a sin den appealed to him at the moment.

Shade said, "Don't worry about Bracket. If he ain't dead, he's got to turn up some place. It's just a question of when and where."

"You got men watchin' the mines real close?"

"He can't get outa Field City nohow."

"But if he's in town, where the hell is he hidin'?"

"Boss, that's Mulloy's end of it. He's got Moriarty and the Swede and Cannon and whoever else he needs. If Mulloy's on the job, Bracket can't hit the street without bein' spotted."

Field took another drink. He seldom drank much whiskey, he was chary of relinquishing complete clarity of mind. "You should have finished him."

"We should've been able to see who it was shot at us. That's where we could get into trouble," said Shade.

"Why in the hell didn't you?"

Shade said, "Look at it from our angle. We took the money belt. We didn't dare fire a shot. None of us is a knife man. We was kickin' the tar outa him. Someone fires a shot at us. It's dark where the shot comes from. Maybe there's more'n one comin' at us. What could we do?"

There was reason in what he said, Field thought. He got up without answering and went into the kitchen. Shade was logical, in fact he was smart, far more clever than Mulloy. Maybe he was too damn smart.

He took another quick drink and fire ran through his veins. He was staring at the curtains which Monty had hung for Mary.

He hadn't realized how deep the iron was in him when it came to the girl. He had thought of her in terms of good relationship among the townsfolk, of a good woman to bear children and make him a solid citizen. The trouble was, he had thought of her too often, now it had become more than he could handle, the way he felt.

He had made his move against Johnny Bracket because of Mary, he realized. He had taken over this ranch because it was intended for her home. He had ordered Johnny killed because of Mary.

He steadied himself. He had built Field City to his specifications, he wanted it that way, he meant to keep it that way. When Johnny Bracket was dead and flung into Deep Canyon there would be an end to opposition. He could handle the mine owners through the laborers and hangers-on who would infest the town. He had nothing to fear if he could only do away with Johnny Bracket. After all, who was there to seek vengeance for a drifter like the Texan?

In the Old Boss Saloon on El Paso Street three men stood against the bar. One was huge and squareheaded and blond. His name was Stoudenmire. Another was medium-sized, dark and of sober demeanor, a man named Jim Gillett. Between them was a lean sixty-year old, with seamy brown face and exceedingly bright brown eyes. He was Joe Bracket.

"It's too damn long between drinks," said Stoudenmire.

"You've had enough, Dallas," Gillett said gently.

"I be goddam, Jim, you're gettin' sour. You're actin' like a goddam preacher."

"Sure, Dallas," said Gillett. He winked at Joe Bracket. "Why don't you go across the street and make the action?"

The big man stared over at the Coliseum, which even at this early hour was crowded with gamesters and women in fancy costume. "Them Manning boys are goin' to get it from me."

"Now, you know those boys are all right. Go on, talk to 'em."

Stoudenmire said, "Well, you bastids won't drink with me, I might's well."

He walked very steadily, leaving the Old Boss. Jim Gillett sighed.

"He's a sudden man."

"He's pistol bait," said Joe Bracket.

"Yeah. So every man has got to die, why not at the end of a Colt?"

"Don't sound like you, Jim. Quittin' the Rangers didn't stick in your craw, did it?"

"No. When Reynolds left, I knew it was time. A man don't get time for anything but police work with the Rangers any more." Gillett paused, then said, "You wanted to ask me somethin'?"

Joe Bracket finished his drink. He indicated a carpet-bag on a nearby deal table. "I'm takin' a trip up no'th."

"One of the boys?"

"Johnny."

"Uh-huh. How's Toole? And Sam?"

"Toole, he's around somewhere. Sam's Marshal in Farwell again. They're always all right."

"Johnny evidently ain't."

"Johnny's got a wowser by the tail."

"Two legged or otherwise?"

"All kinds, I reckon."

"I always cottoned to Johnny. Mean little bastid."

"Mean as a basketful of snakes," said Joe Bracket. "Did you ever know a man named Morgan Field or a Tom Mulloy?"

Jim Gillett scowled. *"Morgan* Field? Big fella, too much around the women?"

"Sounds right, if I can read betwixt the lines of what Johnny writ me."

"Mulloy, he was a deputy here in El Paso." Gillett set his glass down firmly on a damp ring, moved it in a circle. "You mind old Manny Freed?"

"The book-readin' outlaw?"

"The same. He had a sidekick named Jake Field. They called him Lady Killer Field. Mulloy was workin' this end, Freed's gang was holdin' up the express stages, pickin' the big hauls. Then Field got mixed up with a whore named Sally Gore. Manny went to jail, you know, Reynolds got him, and Field was livin' off this little ole Sally."

"Sounds like a real gent."

"Well, there was a jeweler, Sol Kohn. One night he turned up murdered. The killer got everything worth a dime in the store. Mulloy couldn't explain why he didn't nail the guilty party. They fired Mulloy. Field never was seen around El Paso any more."

"I see."

"Sally kilt herself soon after. Nice little whore, she was, too."

"Sounds like this Field is a real one, huh?"

"Why don't Johnny kill him?"

"That's always the trouble with Johnny. He gets delicate at times."

"You thinkin' of doin' it for him?"

Joe Bracket nodded at the carpet-bag. "Got a shotgun busted down in there. Way it seems, Johnny may not be around by the time I get 'way up there. We'll see about it."

"You need any help, lemme know."

"Thanks, Jim." He put money on the bar. "I got to catch that train."

"Okay, Joe."

There was plenty of spring in the step of the aging man as he went toward the depot. He looked at his turnip watch, he had time enough. He saw Stoudenmire, drunk as a bear, coming toward him, waving his arms. He shook his head and walked quicker and turned into the station.

A six-foot young man, dark and saturnine, with sharp eyes, a sharp nose and a dimple in his chin said, "Hiya, Pa."

"Hiya, Toole. Where you come from?"

"Not far. Wells Fargo had some stuff on the wire about trouble in Field City."

"It's the truth."

"This was the nearest station. Anyway, I figured you might have got word."

"The little bastid, you know how he is. You think he ain't got a lick of family feelin', then he gets into a bind and he sends a telegram."

"Good," said Toole. "Got your ticket?"

"Sure, I got my ticket."

"So have I. Let's go." They started toward the train.

As they were ready to mount the steps, Toole asked, "Pa, you reckon we got time?"

"No, I'm afraid not."

"You got that greener in the bag?"

"Yep."

Toole said, "I brought two six-guns in mine."

"Yeah," said Joe Bracket. "Well, shall we take a ride on the choo choo?"

"After you," said Toole. His face was smooth and clear but his eyes were narrow and cruel as he followed his agile father onto the train.

# chapter thirteen

THE THIRD TIME Johnny Bracket woke up he knew at once where he was and that Susan Carter was again at his side. He also knew he was feeling a lot better.

He sat up and she moved to allow him room to drop his legs over the side of the bed. He was stark naked and he wondered which of them had undressed him, hoping it was Madame Victoria, who had seen better and worse and in any case wouldn't care.

Susan Carter said, "I'm glad you can move. It is going to be dangerous here, I'm afraid."

"I'm ready to leave." Johnny tried a smile. "It ain't a fitten place for an engaged man."

She was silent. He looked at her while his head spun around once, then remained steady on his neck and shoulders.

"I got to thank you. I don't know how," he said.

"Never mind the thanks. If I can get out alive, get away from Morg with enough to start over, I'll be satisfied. I'm counting on you."

"If you could get me my duds, it would be a start," he told her. "Man don't feel right without his pants."

"In the cabinet, over there." She rose and went across the room, turning her back.

He hesitated only a fraction of a moment. Then he went to the chest against the wall and found that his underclothing and shirt had been washed and pressed and that his pants had been mended in a couple of places. "Service is great around here." He wobbled a little but managed to dress. "Eight thousand dollars, they got. Lot of money. Borrowed money, at that."

He found his gunbelt with a new Colt resting in the scabbard. He put it on and tried the feel of the weapon. She had turned around and was looking at him.

She said, "Is it all right?"

"It'll do, until I get my own back."

She said, "Shade took your gun."

"Never mind Shade. He's nothin', alone."

"That's right."

He said, "It ain't goin' to be easy, Morg being the Mayor."

"He's out at your place, but men are running back and forth with messages all the time. I'm worried about that telegram Madame Victoria sent your father."

"I'd be more worried if it didn't get delivered."

She said, "Morg is still after your girl, you know. He'd like to get rid of you and have another go at her."

"Sure, he would." He squinted at her. "You jealous of Mary?"

"No. Only . . . I wish things could be different. I wish . . . But they can't ever be, you see?"

"I wouldn't say that."

She said, "I've been watching you ever since you hit town, Johnny Bracket. If it had been you that took me out of the house and helped me, then it might have been different."

He was deeply embarrassed. "I'll do anything I can, you can count on that."

"There's nothing anyone can do. It's too late. People can talk about another chance, starting over, but when you're in as deep as I am, it's just a pipe dream."

"That's no way to believe."

She said, "Morg thought he could change, be a politician, a businessman. Look at him. The first sign of competition, the first time he loses out—over a girl, at that—he goes back to what he always was, a thief and a killer."

"Which nobody can prove."

She said, "I can. I recognized Shade and Frey and Halliday."

"Nobody knows that, I hope?"

"Nobody but you and Madame."

"I'd rather it was only me."

She said, "You've got to slip out of here. You've got to get to your friends at the mines."

"How about Pedro Armindez?"

"At the diggings," she said. "They're all up at the mines."

"Then I'll have to make it alone."

She said, "Tonight, I'll see if I can clear the way."

"Mulloy, the Swede and Cannon will be looking. Who else?"

"A few of the new people. Gunslingers, bums that Mulloy can hire for a dollar and drinks."

"How soon will it be dark?"

"An hour or two. You have time to eat."

"Tell Madame to send up a bottle. Let's you and me have a drink before I go."

"I only drink wine," said Susan, smiling faintly. Then she added, "With a dose of laudanum, most times."

"Yeah, I surmised that," he said soberly. "I'm real sorry about that."

"Don't be. It's easier for me."

He was uncomfortable under her steady gaze. She was strikingly beautiful at times, so lovely that his heart ached for what she might have been. "All right, wine. I'll drink a bottle of wine with you."

He remembered what his father used to say, "Appearance, son, can be deceptive." Here he was, about to dine and wine with a whore in a house of assignation, yet never had he been more innocent. He hoped Mary would never know.

Mary Jones was struggling to keep her temper. Things had been going wrong all day. They would never make Field City before sundown unless the wagons began creaking their way southward.

Lonely said, "I'm real sorry, Mary. The wagons had to be loaded. There just ain't enough help."

"People are too busy minding their own business," she retorted. "They haven't got time to pitch in and help. Johnny found the gold but that doesn't matter."

"Well, Amsy helped. He's goin' to ride in with us, too, now that Monty is out of it."

She looked at Monty, unconscious on a blanket, blind drunk. They were going to put him behind the high seat of one of the ore wagons and take him along. She felt nothing but pity for the Englishman.

Randy Holt, soiled and weary, came to them and said, "We can take off, now. How do you want us to travel, Mr. Jones?"

"We'll put Monty in the first wagon. You drive. Amsy and Mary will bring up in the second wagon. Pedro can ride ahead and scout. I'll take the rear guard."

"Why should they hit us? The ore is no good to them without its being milled and refined."

Mary said, "If Johnny is dead he won't attack us. If Johnny's alive—maybe."

"How do you figure?"

"If he's dead, Morg Field can bide his time and take over what he pleases. Everything. I know it, now. He can do it."

Lonely said, "If he made the play against Johnny, and Johnny is still alive, then Morg's in for it. He made a mistake if he didn't get Johnny killed."

Randy Holt said, "I see. Yes, I believe you're right. But shouldn't Mary stay here, where she can be safe?"

She said, "No."

Then he knew she was going in because of Johnny, because she could no longer stand the uncertainty, because she didn't want to live without knowing. It sickened him and it also hardened him. He helped put Monty in back of the seat and climbed up and took the reins. They were using heavy ore wagons with huge wheels and there were draft horses to pull them, big-footed animals bought from farmers, new to this country.

He was young enough to dream, guiltily, that Johnny was dead, that Morg Field was defeated and that Randy Holt, an honest, hardworking young mine owner, was suitable to court Mary Jones. Oh, it would take time. It wouldn't happen in a week, a month. Within a year, maybe, when the mill was built and the ore was running through and Randy Holt was acknowledged a brilliant young man. Mama wouldn't have anything to say about it, either . . .

The dream faltered and hung dry on the vision of Mama, then burgeoned as the wagon creaked and rolled down the rocky road.

Word came to Field that afternoon, a note written in Mulloy's scratchy script, delivered by an Indian boy who immediately vanished westward.

"Madame Victoria sent telegram to Joe Bracket, El Paso. Damn operator never told, had to find it myself. Am moving onto Madame pronto."

Field said, "Damn it, Bracket is alive. I'll go in."

"You want us?"

"No. You saddle up and ride out to the trail. Cover the mines, just in case he gets away. Check on everybody."

"What about Madame?"

Field said, "We got to go easy, there. Madame owns a lot of tinhorns and flash boys. I'll take care of Madame in due time."

Shade said, "I still think we better go in with you."

"No. I want that trail covered. The men you got out there don't understand the way it is."

"You mean you want Bracket dead and in Deep Canyon if he comes our way?"

"That's right, Shade."

"Makes good sense." He turned to the others. "Saddle up, Frey. Halliday, you make sure of guns and shells. I'll catch up the black for you, boss."

Field went into the parlor and put on his gun belt. He

took a long look around the room, now somewhat awry and soiled, still retaining marks of the good taste of Monty Carruthers. It was enough to heat up his rage against Johnny Bracket to a boiling point.

The combination of hate and whiskey lasted him into town. He drove the black stallion down Main Street across the railway tracks. Then he was halted, stunned, by the sight of people milling, the sound of men yelling.

Mulloy met him, sweating, befuddled. Field swung down from the saddle, feeling the first doubts, scowling, angry. He looked toward Madame Victoria's place and saw the tall woman in the doorway, a shotgun cradled in her arms. Behind her were indistinct figures, standing firm, silent against the crowd noise. Moriarty, the Swede and Cannon faced her, irresolute. Darkness was falling and someone lit a flaring brand.

A drunk yelled, "Go on, Swede, knock her down. Or is she too much woman for you?"

The big Swede wagged his head, looking for Mulloy. The other deputies stirred but took no action.

"What the hell do you mean, stirring up a fuss like this?" Field demanded. "Why didn't you go in quiet and look for him?"

"She was waitin' for us," said Mulloy.

"Then why didn't you take her quick and get it over with?"

"You better come and look, Morg," said Mulloy. He was subdued and worried. As they went forward, he fell a step behind, pulling his hat down over his eyes, yellow teeth biting at his moustache.

The drunk spotted them and hooted, "Here comes the Mayor, he'll lay her down. Whoops, Mayor!"

There were catcalls and intermingling shouts of, "The Madame's right, where's your Court Order?"

"You got no right of search or seizure."

"Mulloy ain't the whole world and all."

"Madame Shotgun, that's her name."

There were many people from the Mexican quarters in the mob, Field saw at once. They were not making much noise, but they were scattered in strategic places. He recognized Jose, the laborer and Manuelito, the carpenter. Mulloy had succeeded in stirring up a hornet's nest.

He came opposite the door and paused. He said reasonably in a loud voice, "I don't know what's going on here, but it'll be settled in a minute or two. Why don't you all go about your business and let the law take its course?"

"Mayor Field's law, Mulloy's law," said someone in Spanish accents.

Mulloy whispered in his ear, "Better take a good look, Morg."

He turned and went closer to the front door of the establishment. Madame Victoria surveyed him coldly, her finger on the trigger of the shotgun. Behind her a lean gambler was holding a rifle. Morg stared at the third figure.

His blood ran cold, then hot. For a moment his breath was gone, then he swelled with rage.

Susan Carter looked coolly back at him. She had a small revolver in her right hand. With her left she adjusted a lock of her dark hair which had become disarranged.

Madame Victoria said, "Send your gunslingers away, Mayor. The town won't hold still for illegal search and entry."

He choked. Susan had not altered expression. She was staring at him with her hot, Indian eyes as though he was a stranger. He knew this was a moment of danger, he knew what he had to do. Yet he wanted to draw his gun and shoot, driving bullet after bullet at them, making sure of all of them, making deadly sure of Susan Carter. It took him a long moment to get hold of himself.

Then he turned to the crowd. He said clearly, calmly, "That's right. There's to be no illegal procedures in this town while I'm Mayor. Now. Go on, break it up."

"We're not goin' 'till your deputies go and leave 'em alone," howled a hard rock miner in rough clothing. "We seen your kind before."

Field said, "No harm will come to anyone if you disperse. Mob action is as wrong as police action."

Mulloy and the deputies stood at his side. Field whispered, "Send the men around back, Tom. One by one, but get there, fast."

"I already got men at the back."

"Never mind. Do like I say and hurry."

Mulloy spoke to the Swede and Moriarty beckoned to Cannon. They left slowly, reluctantly, while the crowd hooted at them. Morg turned back to Madame Victoria.

"You'd better let me in," he said. "A mob can cause a lot of damage even if it is on your side."

She nodded. "But be careful with your hands, Mayor. This shotgun's got an easy trigger."

She stepped aside. He had to brush close to Susan Carter as he entered. It seemed as though both were on fire, that a conflagration would result. The door closed behind them and they were in the small bar, with its piano and chandelier brought in from St. Louis and the dais where the girls sang or danced for patrons who were not inclined to go upstairs.

The tinhorn, a very thin man, remained in the background, gripping the rifle, looking to Madame Victoria for aid and comfort. There was a scared bartender and the Professor who played the piano, quite drunk and unconcerned. Madame did not relinquish the shotgun.

Morg Field faced them and made his voice quiet. "I'm not sure I savvy this play . . . Susan?"

"I decided I didn't want the house," she said. "Madame doesn't need competition."

"You decided?"

"You told me to talk with Madame."

"Oh. Yes, I did, didn't I?" He kept his hand away from his gun. He concealed his anger as best he could, speaking to Madame. "She came out of a house you wouldn't put your nose into. She takes laudanum. She's trouble. You don't want her."

"I'll take my chances," said Madame. "What I want to know, why did you send your goddam Marshal here to take her away?"

"You've got it all wrong." Then he realized that it was better if they thought that was the reason for Mulloy's action. He corrected himself, "Well, Susan was my girl. It didn't seem right for her to be here."

"But it would be all right in a house of her own?"

"That's different. You know it's different, Madame."

"No different if somebody like you is the owner. I've made her a deal to help me out."

"Is that right, Susan?"

She said, "That's right." She knew Mulloy was looking for Johnny Bracket, and Madame knew it, but if Morg wanted to play it this way, perhaps it was for the best. It gave Johnny more time.

Morg Field shrugged. "If that's what you want, I can't

stop you. Let's forget it and have a drink. That shotgun makes me a little nervous, Madame. I'll buy."

She made a circular motion with the twin muzzles of the weapon and said, "Set 'em up, Jerry. Makes me nervous, too, Mister Field. I can't miss with this thing at close range."

"Why should you want to fight me? I'm a business man, you can dicker with me."

Madame laughed unpleasantly. The faded blonde girl called Mona came in and said, "The crowd's gone, Madame. Only a couple of bums hangin' around."

"All right. You and your man skiddoo." He watched as the thin gambler put his arm around Mona and led her away toward the stairs. "Love in a tub and the bottom fell out," she continued. "Every little thing helps, sometimes. He never had guts before."

Susan was across the room, the revolver still in evidence. The bartender shakily poured drinks. Madame managed hers without relinquishing her shotgun. Morg Field put money on the bar and held his drink in his right hand, the side on which he wore his Colts. Susan refused to drink.

And now, in this moment, she knew at last what it was to be an Indian, a real, thoroughgoing Indian. She felt the Wings of Death, the Last Deep Shadow soaring nearby. Not only in this room, she knew, but in the county. Denied too long, the hovering Black Bird was coming to claim his prey. No amount of mission training could eradicate from her this prescience, this burning and conclusive knowledge. She almost lifted the gun to fire at Morgan Field, but here her Christian schooling did indeed interfere.

Johnny Bracket, ensconced in a stall in Amsy Buchanan's stable, said, "It ain't right to leave the women with them."

Diego, the faithful carpenter responded, "Señor, these are whores, wise and brave in the ways of man."

"They saved my life."

"Of a certainty, they did. May the Virgin bless them. May they become again as other women. But you must go to the mines and rally your people, Señor. We need you. We are too poor, too cowardly to fight the Señor Jefe. It is only you who can make us strong."

Johnny said, "If I get outa here alive, maybe I can do something. Maybe. I don't know."

"You must get out," said Diego. "Take the horse and go, pronto."

The horse was Amsy's best, all saddled and ready, a good enough hack. It would not be wise to ride his own mount. He was dressed in Diego's clothing to resemble a Mexican, peaked sombrero, serape of many colors to hide the familiar shape of him. Time was running short, he must go through the byways of town and to Mary and Lonely and Monty and the others. Just naming them to himself gave him confidence.

He said, "Okay, here goes nothin'."

He drew the serape about his shoulders, tapped the conical sombrero firmly in place. He made sure his hands were free to reach his revolver as he went toward the horse. Diego made a gesture with the discarded hat, his teeth showing in dim lantern light.

"Hasta luego, compadre," he said softly.

Then Mulloy's voice said from the yard, "Get him!"

Johnny swung the cape aside, drawing the Colts. There were several shots. Diego cried out and fell against the stable wall. They had mistaken him for Johnny because of Johnny's hat.

It gave him a moment to swing around. He fired at the flashes of the pistols, then as he moved a light from Madame Victoria's suddenly opened rear door gave him a view of Mulloy and he steadied himself, shooting low for the belt buckle, then turning, moving as lead fanned past his ears, keeping away from the horse because he knew he would need the horse.

He saw Mulloy go backwards as though yanked by a lariat and heard other voices of the crowd Morg Field had sent around to the back. He bent low and emptied the Colts, then he had to run for it. He made a flying leap into the saddle as the horse neighed and reared.

He had trouble getting the rifle out of the scabbard, but the circling, scared horse made of him a poor target. No bullet touched him but his sore ribs hurt and the pain made him angrier, if possible. He knew Diego was dead and when he finally got the rifle loose he was reckless of it, spraying the yard as he fought to control the horse with one hand, holding the butt of the rifle against his body, shooting until it, too, was empty, then spurring out of the stable yard onto Main Street, people scattering as he drove the horse over the railway tracks and out on the road to the diggings at Lost Peak.

Diego dead, now there would be reprisals in the Mexican quarters, the town in an uproar, he thought. Diego of the clever hands, who had helped him out of Madame's house while his friends demonstrated at the front door, who had given his life in hopes that his people might gain a precious thing known as "freedom."

There would be war now, with Mulloy also downed and Morg Field demanding that Johnny be arrested for murder. There was lynching material in the charge, there was chance enough that the uncertain populace would be coerced or swindled into following the Mayor.

He rode, uphill, saving the horse, wanting desperately to be with Mary and Lonely and the others, his friends, who had as much at stake as he. He reloaded his guns as he rode, wondering how many he had cut down, not regretful at taking life this time, not thinking of anything except that Morgan Field and all with him must be, for the common good, destroyed.

When the first shot sounded, Susan Carter was emotionally and physically lost in the cloud of doom. Mona's weak, high voice screamed "They got Johnny," and she knew it was the end of everything she wanted. She had already been conditioned to tragedy, the Indian gods had prepared her. But the suddenness with which it came froze her to the wall, kept her speechless and actionless.

Even when Morg Field, taking quick and canny advantage of Madame's start and withdrawn attention, struck out, Susan could not raise the small pistol to fire at him. She saw Madame go down, bleeding, losing her grip on the shotgun, saw the bartender dive for safety, craven to the last.

It had been a bad life, right from the start, from the first seduction through the succession of bagnios, through alcohol and drugs and then through the brief time when she had believed in and loved Morgan Field. It seemed to her that it was all perfectly useless, that nothing added up, nothing produced nothing. If she could lift the revolver and press the trigger she might accomplish at least one deed before she departed. She might rid the world of the Mayor of Field City.

She struggled with herself. She saw Field's face as he

wheeled around, the muzzle of his pistol wet with Madame Victoria's blood. She saw him recognize that she held the gun, held his life in her hand.

She knew what was going to happen. She faced him, the weapon half-engaged, willing herself to shoot but knowing the gods had finally given up on her, that there was no place on earth or beyond where she could find surcease, that life and after-life held nothing for the half-Indian girl who was doomed from conception.

When Field's bullet hit her in the breast she thought that it was good that he had not disfigured her face, that she would haunt the country to which she was going without disfiguration. All that she had ever possessed was her beauty and it would be shameful to have that destroyed in the end.

The second shot she did not even feel as it ploughed into her heart, stilling it forever, releasing her from the cloud of doom, from all the tortures of her living. She was sliding down the wall, into blackness when he realized what he had done and ran toward her, saying, "No . . . I thought you were going to shoot . . . I didn't mean to kill you!"

But the reason he said that, of course, was not from remorse, he had wished her dead many times. It was because he knew he could not kill Madame Victoria and the bartender and Mona and her thin gambler and everyone who would know that he had murdered a woman. And he knew that even the lowest scum who infested the dives of Field City would not countenance this killing, not from the Mayor, not especially from a political figure. A tinhorn or a pimp might shoot his woman, no one cared, but Morgan Field could not do so and survive.

He knew it as he knelt beside her, cursing her, and if he needed more proof it was in the words of semi-conscious Madame Victoria, who lay half behind the bar, blood streaming down her face from the scalp cut he had inflicted.

She said, "Susan got you, Mr. Mayor. She got you as sure as if she fired into your guts, goddam you."

Then Madame relapsed into oblivion. The barkeep had not moved from his prone position; he was praying, a strange sound in this place at this time.

Morg Field straightened and ran out back, where the firing had stopped. He wanted to see Johnny Bracket dead. He stepped over a prone body, paused, looked hard, bent low.

There were moans from shadows in the stable yard. But

the man lying under Field's regard did not protest his wounds. He was stone dead. One bullet had neatly clipped a corner from the star upon his vest. His moustache was stained with crimson, his mouth was parted to show the yellow teeth. Tom Mulloy was gone to his reward, revolver in hand, boots on.

Field straightened and Moriarty cried out, "In the barn. We got him, but somebody shot us all to hell. I need a doctor, Boss."

In the stable there was Johnny Bracket's hat and the dead Diego. Morg Field took a deep breath.

He went to the corral where the black was still saddled and waiting, as he had ordered. Susan was dead, a Mexican-American was dead, Mulloy was dead. Field City was no longer his town, because Johnny Bracket was not dead.

He turned toward the bank, rode the back way. People were milling in the streets, there was no law, no one to take charge. Simon Jarret would become either man or mouse tonight in his semi-official position as candidate for office. There was only one possible procedure for Morgan Field.

He systematically looted the bank of every available piece of cash, using sturdy canvas sacks which he packed in his saddle bags. He would go to the ranch where he would gather Shade and Frey and Halliday and take off to the West. Denver, San Francisco, any place would do, with the money and men behind him he could start again.

He would always regret Field City. He had owned it, lock, stock and barrel, until he had made one mistake. Just one small error in judgment, he thought, fastening the saddle bags securely, mounting the black stallion. If he had not backed Johnny Bracket, all would have been well.

He heard the wild, lonely hoot of the evening train, thought for a moment that perhaps he should get on it and desert Shade and the others, change his name and settle down as a man of means on the Coast or in South America where Courtright and the others had gone to flee the United States law.

Then he knew he could not do so, because there was still Johnny Bracket. Before he left he must, with Shade and the two gunmen, find Bracket and kill him. A long range job, he thought, riding the back, dark ways as Field City rioted, any kind of ambush, anything to destroy the man who had taken his town away from him.

Joe Bracket stood on the railroad platform holding a yellow flimsy carpet-bag in a hand more accustomed to rope, leather or branding iron and said in wonderment, "It beats me all to hell how they do it. Sendin' you a telegram and you ridin' on a damn train."

Toole said, "Pa, they send it to a station ahead, then when the train pulls in they hand it to the conductor and he walks through the cars until he finds you or don't find you, as the case may be."

"Yeah. That has got to be the right of it. I swan to ginney, you young fellas get to know everything. Now how in hell did Sam get word?"

"Well, tell you the truth, I sent him a telegram to Farwell."

"Oh, I see." Joe Bracket scowled. "Didn't think I could handle it, you two, huh? First you, now Sam."

"Pa, it isn't that. Johnny is in a real jackpot. That man Field is smart, he's Manny Freed smart and gun smart and crooked smart. You know Johnny."

"Never had nothin' against Johnny. It was him started it, when I married. I figure Johnny right able."

"I didn't mean it that way." It was hard to get along with the old man, Toole thought. No wonder Johnny took off before it was time, before the brothers could organize and show the kid the ropes. "All I mean is, with Sam we got an experienced lawman and a good gun hand."

Joe put the carpet-bag on a wooden bench and opened it. He took out a shotgun stock and a foreshortened barrel and began putting it together by the uncertain light of the lamps. "And here we are, waitin' for Sam instead of gettin' to it. Why can't we go into town and start lookin' around?"

Toole said, "Because Sam might arrive and not know where we're at. Anyway, he said to wait at the station."

"I hate waitin'." He loaded the shotgun with buckshot. "There seems to be a heap of noise over yonder, below the tracks."

The telegraph operator came out and whined, "There's been shootin' and riotin' and what-all. Mayor Field should be puttin' it down, by now. Can't understand why Mulloy and the deputies ain't stopped it."

"That's Tom Mulloy, from Texas way?"

"Our Town Marshal."

Joe Bracket said, "From what I hear, he couldn't stop a church social. Unless there was a fast dollar in it."

"Mulloy's a law officer, a good one," said the operator. "He's Mayor Field's right hand. He keeps the greasers in place. He makes everybody toe the mark. He's on the right side hereabouts, Mister Whoever-you-are."

Joe turned slowly, the shotgun held carelessly in his gnarled hands. "Mister Bracket, father of Johnny Bracket, that's whoever-I-am. You got any remarks to make about my son, or anybody connected with my son?"

The operator retreated into his office, then found nerve to say through the window, "Johnny Bracket's either dead or hidin' out. You better look out for Mulloy and the Mayor and the law in this here town, Mr. Bracket."

"Oh, I'll look out for it, all right," said Joe. "Dead or hidin', eh? Sam better get here pretty quick, Toole."

"Yes," said the handsomest Bracket. "I reckon he had, at that. Just a little while longer, Pa. He's comin' horseback, you got to allow him a little time."

When the familiar figure finally appeared, spurring a weary horse, it was from the direction of town. Joe cursed as he came near enough to be recognized.

Sam was the biggest of the Brackets. He was six feet six in his stockings and wide as a barn door. He dismounted however, with the agility of a circus acrobat.

"Got here a bit early," he explained. "Went into town to see what was doin'. Kinda got trapped."

His father said heatedly, "You're wearin' your star. Damn if you ain't always got to be a lawman."

Sam said self-consciously, "It ain't official outside Farwell, but the way things are here, it seemed a good idea to pin it on."

"What way are things here? What about Johnny?"

"Johnny's been hurt but he got clean away. Seems he shot a few people. The Marshal, fella named Mulloy, and a couple of deputies."

"Mulloy, huh? Now, it does seem a shame I never got to meet up with that fascinatin' fella," said Joe.

"But what about Johnny?" Toole demanded.

"Well, I found old Madame Victoria, remember her?"

Toole grinned despite his worriment. "I sure do."

"Seems Mayor Field belted her with his little old pistol. Then, near as we can tell, he looted the bank and headed out of town."

"Horseback?"

"Yeah. Madame says he must be goin' to pick up his bunch. She says he's got a bad bunch."

"You know what direction he's pickin' up these bad boys?"

"I know." Sam hesitated. "Look, Johnny's got a start. I figure him to be all right for an hour or two. Now, here in town there is a barber named Jarret; he is trying very hard to hold down the lid and he is not doin' very good."

Pa said, "I want a horse and I want after Johnny."

"Sure, Pa, but this town, it's Johnny's town, sort of. Fella named Jose, a big strong Mex fella, he's tryin' to control his people, the tinhorns are actin' up, the bums and crumbs are riotin' in the streets."

"And you couldn't handle it?"

"Now, Pa, I heard the train come in. I couldn't keep you waitin', could I? Besides, the three of us can do it a lot quicker'n just me."

Mollified, Joe hefted the shotgun. "Well, get on with it. You and your sense of law and order. I don't know what I ever done to get me a damn lawman for a son."

The affair on the trail was, Lonely thought anguishedly, mainly his own fault, although circumstances were against people riding the wagons and ill luck played a great part. The fact that Rag Shade was drinking was fatal.

Pedro Armindez, good man, was not a plainsman; he should not have been riding scout in advance. He never saw Shade nor the other two who watched from above as he rode by, then came in on him silently and knocked him from the saddle, braining him where he lay because he tried to get his rifle into play, dragging him off the road, silencing his horse, rolling him under a bush, where he drained away his life without ever knowing it.

When that deed was done the bottle went from hand to hand until it was empty. Shade knew that if there was an advance guard there must be someone riding rear guard and he acted accordingly. He let the wagons go through, laid in wait for Lonely, jumped him from a tall rock, knocked him out.

Then they rode on the wagons.

Here they could not know that Randy Holt was wrapped in dreams of heroism, exalted by the hope that he would one day possess the object of his love. They only saw the callow youth dive for his rifle behind the seat. They lost their heads for a moment as Amsy Buchanan, hearing Randy shout, went into action with a lever action Winchester. It was growing quite dark and Amsy missed.

Shade shot Holt, so that the boy flopped around on the seat. The horses, stung and puzzled by the slapping of the reins took off down the steep trail, the bits in their teeth, traces slack, wheels trying to catch horses, horses racing beyond their capacity, on a trail not made for swift motion, but the wagon remaining upright by some miracle, even while Randy Holt lolled, fingers clutching his body where the blood ran from a hole in his skin, not believing it, not yet quite loose from his dream of glory.

They could have caught the wagon, but Amsy was bothering them and there was the girl, Mary Jones, and they didn't want to kill her, knowing that Morg Field would certainly never forgive them for such an act. They circled like Indians, taking pot shots, making Amsy miss in the darkness.

They finally got him, one way or another. They moved in very fast and Shade finished him with a pistol shot while Frey and Halliday secured the girl, who fought them like a treed catamount.

Then, when they had subdued her as gently as possible, they went back and found Lonely alive and they tied him up and took stock.

Shade said, "Never meant to kill them folks. It just kinda happened."

The whiskey was dying in all of them. "Morg may not like this."

Shade said, "Well, hell. What can we do? Frey, you drive the wagon."

"Where we goin'?"

"Back to the ranch. Check with Morg."

"But hell, the woman and all?"

"That wagon down the road, it's no use goin' after it now, with them people dead. We'll make it to the ranch and see what the boss says."

"It's mighty tetchy, Rag."

"Well, this here is the gal Morg was after. Maybe he'll be glad to see her, at that."

"Mebbe."

Shade was feeling better already, now that his mind settled on the one thing he felt he knew about. "There's that fancy bedroom and everything. He was mighty put out when he seen that. Havin' the gal there, it might make a difference, see what I mean?"

"I dunno. There's the people in town to think about. People don't like anything like this."

Shade said, "Mulloy and them has got the town in hand. Bracket must be done for by now. What the hell's to worry about?"

"I jest don't like it, Rag," said Frey.

"Like it or not, that's the way she blows," said Shade. "Come on, put the old man in the wagon and we'll head for the ranch. Then we'll see how it comes out."

They picked up Lonely, who pretended to be unconscious, and stowed him in the wagon alongside Mary, both tied with lariats. Frey got on the seat and headed the team of horses toward the Jenkins place. Mary did not weep, which was no surprise to Lonely. There comes a time, he knew, which is beyond tears.

## chapter fourteen

THE SOUND WAS like a distant call of thunder in the night. Johnny Bracket, riding the edge of the road to the mines, felt it coming nearer as the earth trembled. He swung abruptly toward the advancing danger. Horses exhaled tortured breath, sparks flew from hooves, the wagon swerved, rocked, hung an instant, then went over.

Johnny came to earth with knife drawn, running, getting to the struggling, panting team, slashing at straps, finally freeing them. They stood, as trained work animals will, heaving, wild-eyed but reassured by his clucking sounds. The stars had begun to shine and there was a hint of moon from behind a cloud bank. Johnny went curiously to the wagon seat, pulled himself up.

Randy Holt's face was no more than six inches away. The boy's mouth opened, then shut as his eyes closed, then opened again. He was propped against the blanketed seat, his hands clutching, braced hard, his blood thick around him.

He said, "Johnny? That you Johnny?"

"Randy. What happened, Randy?"

"Morg Field's men."

"They shot you?"

"Shot hell out of . . . us."

"Us? You and who else, Randy?"

"All of us . . . Mary . . . Mary was with Amsy Buchanan . . . other wagon."

"There were two wagons?"

"Two . . . Pedro . . . Lonely . . . Where are they?"

A wipe-out, Johnny thought. A complete finish. Morg Field had determined on annihilation. Kill them all and answer questions later.

He said, "Monty?"

"He was . . . with me . . . in wagon." The voice faded, then came stronger. "Johnny?"

"Yes. I'm here."

"We were scared you were dead. Now . . . how many are dead?"

"I don't know, Randy."

The boy whimpered a little, then said clearly, "Me . . . I'm dead, Johnny."

The hand grip loosened. The face slid away from Johnny, the body collapsed like an empty sack, the will finally denied, all going away into a small bundle of rough clothing on the downside of an overturned wagon.

Johnny walked around. Shock and grief mingled with fear as he bent and picked up the slight form of the former bank clerk. Gold ore rattled beneath his boots and he wished fervently that he had never kicked loose the nugget on that day which seemed so long ago. It would have been better to turn the ranch back to Field, to marry and begin again; anything would have been better than this.

Then Monty's voice said, "Johnny. Is he dead, Johnny?"

He almost dropped the boy, spinning in the starlight. Monty was leaning against a tree, oddly misshapen.

"He's dead. Where did you come from?"

"From hell, Johnny. From the hell of all drunks."

"You don't drink, Monty." He put the body down gently.

"I drank. I was passed out. I woke up when the shooting started. Partially, that is, only partially. They had wrapped me well against the night air." Monty choked. "If I were sober I could have handled the rifle that lay across my chest. Randy was killed reaching for it, you know."

Johnny said, "That's no use, Monty. Leave it alone."

"I was drunk."

"You better tell me all about it." Johnny drew a deep breath. "We'll have to go up trail and see about Amsy and Pedro."

"Were they alive, this couldn't have happened in such fashion," said Monty. "No use, they have Mary, they will be at the ranch, you know. They could not go into town with Mary."

"Yes. The ranch." But Johnny shook his head stubbornly. "Amsy, Pedro, Lonely . . . Got to check out on 'em. You can ride one of the team. We've got to move."

"My fault," Monty said in a dry, cracking whisper. "I was drunk again, God help me."

"The horse," said Johnny. "Hurry."

Monty was able to help remove the harness, except for the bridle. Johnny put him on the horse's broad back and they started up the trail. The moon was becoming brighter, lacy through the tall trees. It was a fine, starlit night but neither of them knew it.

Morgan Field rode the black stallion into the yard and a wrangler named Spud came to take its head. Shade came out of the shadows. Field swung the saddlebags loose, gripping them tight.

"Have you got another man outside?" he demanded.

"Eggers is watchin' the lane."

Field said, "There's hell to pay in town. Bracket got clean away. Mulloy and the Swede are dead."

"Mulloy, huh?" Shade sighed. "Better come inside, boss."

"I tell you, we got to make tracks out of here. Don't you understand? I've got enough to take us a long way." He rattled the saddlebags.

"Better come in. We had a happenstance, too."

There was enough meaning in Shade's tone to send him stalking into the house, through the kitchen, into the parlor. Frey and Halliday did not meet his glance. He stopped dead, staring.

Lonely was tied to a chair against the wall. Mary lay on the bed—he could see her through the open door—hands and feet secured by torn sheet, skirts disarranged, her burnished hair loose and flowing. He stepped toward her, horrified, then suddenly elated to see her helpless, lying there. Her eyes met his and he stopped dead.

Indian eyes, blue eyes, both held the same contempt and hatred for him. For a long moment he stood there, holding his plunder in his hands, absorbing the loathing which the girl conveyed without words, without grimace, through her eyes.

Then he said to Shade, "Can you depend on those two out there?"

"They like money."

Field went into the kitchen, away from the gaze of Mary and Lonely Jones. He took bills from the saddlebag and said, "Pay them enough to make them fight, not enough to run away with."

Shade said, "I thought you said we were to vamoos."

"You didn't get them all. If someone got to town, they'll be on my heels. Put one man out to watch. The other with a rifle in the stable."

Shade turned to the silent Frey and Halliday, hesitated, feeling their reproach but knowing their loyalty, then went outside with the money. Field stood a moment, pondering. If they rode out and were overtaken he knew what it would mean. Johnny Bracket would never let him go to trial.

If they stayed and only Bracket came with whoever was left of his friends there might be a chance for a victory before flight.

He said, "Douse the lights. Get out close to the house and watch for Bracket or the Britisher or any of them. Shoot if they come into your sights."

Frey and Halliday went without a word, taking their rifles from against the wall, disapproving but committed. Field went back into the parlor and blew out the lamp. There was a fire in the fireplace which gave a small light.

He said, "Well, Lonely, I tried to make it come out right."

"You tried hell."

"Johnny Bracket. He fouled it up."

"You didn't need his help."

"I picked up your son's town and put it on its feet. Everything would have been all right. You'd have had to see it my way."

Lonely said, "Not even you can believe that."

Field found a bottle and poured a drink. "Mary would have seen it, wouldn't you, Mary?"

"Is Johnny dead?" she asked, her voice strained and strangely dissonant. "Just tell me that."

"Johnny's alive," said Field. "He's out there some place. You may have to buy his future, but right now he's alive."

Mary said, "If he's alive, then you'll finally pay."

"Amen," said Lonely.

Field drank again. He said half to himself, "I could set fire to the place and ride out. They'd never catch me. Why don't I just do that?"

"Why don't you?" Lonely asked. "Haven't you got the nerve?"

"You people are crazy, tied up there, talking to me like that. What difference now if I kill you?"

"None," said Lonely. "Either way, you hang whether Johnny gets you or the law gets you."

"You believe that." Field laughed shortly without humor. "You really believe that."

"I know it."

"Whatever else happens, let me tell you one thing, both of you. I'm getting out of here and I'm taking everything I need with me," he shouted. The rage was beginning to build in him again. He needed that anger, that fire to burn him, to spur him to action. "I've got you and when Bracket learns about that, I'll go free."

Lonely said, "Let's just see what happens, huh? Meanwhile, get it in your head, Morg . . . we won't beg nor holler nor kneel. Just keep that straight."

Field walked across the room. He swung his right arm. He knocked the old man and the chair over onto the floor.

Lonely looked up and said, "Now I suppose you'll go in and beat on Mary. It augurs, you're that kind."

Field tipped the whiskey bottle and swallowed hard. Shade came in the rear door and he was grateful for the interruption. He went into the kitchen and closed the door.

Mary called softly, "You all right, Grandpa?"

"I ain't exactly comfortable," said Lonely. "But I sure am alive and ready to kick."

"Johnny's alive," she said.

"How you goin' to believe him?"

"Johnny's alive. We'll get out of this."

"Don't get your hopes too high. Remember Morg's always got some scheme goin'."

"Johnny'll find us. I know he will."

Lonely closed his eyes. It was hideously uncomfortable, lying on his side, tied to the chair. He worked at the fastenings but Shade had done a workmanlike job.

Not that it would do any good to get loose without a weapon. Shade and his men and Morg were on the kill tonight. There was no mistaking it.

Field City, he thought, the dream of his only son, was doomed unless Johnny Bracket could save it. He, Lonely Jones, had started a fire and failed to keep it under control. It was a harrowing thought which he tried hard to put from his mind as he struggled fruitlessly with his bonds.

Johnny Bracket said, "Amsy, Pedro, Randy Holt, how many more? Just you and me left free, the drunk and the drifter."

Monty said, "Steady does it, old boy." He was taking strength from Johnny's distraction. "Not too close to the house, you know."

They had secured the horses before ascending the hillside which led to the ranch. The mountains provided a backdrop to dreariness, there was no light in the house, only a drift of smoke from the chimney.

Johnny said, "If he's got Mary and Lonely in there we can't go shootin'."

"He'll have men around the outside. He's a clever one," said Monty.

They were armed with the rifle Randy had not managed, Amsy's pistol and a shotgun which Pedro had carried. The dead faces of their friends swam in Johnny's consciousness. His ribs ached, his legs felt heavy as lead.

"A man on the road, I think," said Monty. "One in the stable for surprise, wouldn't you say?"

"If I could get close enough, I'd take a chance. Better than leaving Mary with him." Yet Monty was making sense and through his confused anger and agony he was beginning to listen.

"If we had a rope, might make it down the hill at the rear, mightn't we? They wouldn't expect us to come in that way, would they?"

"Rope. Why didn't we bring a rope?"

"I believe I did," said Monty meekly. "From the wagon. I'll get it, shall I?"

He was gone toward the tree where they had left the horses. Johnny crept closer to the ranch house. His head was beginning to clear. If he could get in a shot with the rifle, he could reduce the forces which held the place. Yet he was afraid that a shot might bring reprisals upon Mary and Lonely. He had no illusions regarding the status of Morg Field's mind at this moment.

At that second the guard in the road skylined himself, a perfect target against the moonlight. Johnny's finger was on the trigger, all the anger in him boiled up. That was his house, the place he had earned, that he had, with Monty, rebuilt for Mary. Now it was stolen, held against him by force.

All of him stiffened, he took his finger from the curved steel of the trigger, he lay relaxed at last, waiting for Monty. Killing wasn't enough, there had been too much shooting and braining without reasoning, now was the time to think before acting.

He heard sound behind him and whirled. He heard Monty's voice, saw that there were men with him, scurried like a snake, elbows and knees, rifle at ready.

Someone said, "Johnny, where you at?"

He lined up the familiar figure, almost dropped the gun. "Pa!" Then he whispered, "Keep it quiet, can't you?"

"That's our Johnny," said Joe Bracket. "Ornery as ever."

Toole and Sam crouched as he came to them, looking gravely at him, nodding, not offering words until he had spoken, as if they had parted only hours before.

He said, "I'm right glad to see you. We think they got my girl and her grandpa in there. Must be four, five, maybe six of 'em."

"Your man Field looted the bank," said Joe. "Took us a bit of time to figure things out. The town's quiet, now."

"Then he's got a fortune in cash with him," said Johnny. "He took eight thousand and over from me."

"Where in tarnation you get that much money, son?" asked Joe Bracket. "You stealin' these days?"

"No, and it's a long story," said Johnny. "Thing is, if he's got Mary we can't fight him."

Monty said, "I found the rope, you know."

"I can get around back." Johnny spoke to his father and brothers. "Monty, here, is an engineer. He can handle the rope. You watch from here, huh?"

"Where at you goin' to be, son?"

He explained about the bluff behind the house, how they

had built in its shelter long ago, how he and Monty had rebuilt, how they knew every nook and cranny of the land and the outbuildings.

"You goin' down on a rope? You'll need coverin' fire if somethin' goes wrong."

"Well, you all didn't come here for a family reunion, did you?"

"Mean as a sidewinder on a frosty day," said Joe Bracket. "Give us an idea of the way the geography lays."

Monty did so in clipped, accurate accents, while Johnny coiled the rope about his middle. It was a nice, supple lariat, a bit worn from use at the mine, but strong enough, he thought. He was remembering the terrain of the steep bluff behind the house, picturing the place they could get a good bite that he might be able to slip down behind the barn. Further than that he did not have to think; from then on it would be action dictated by events.

When Monty had finished, Joe Bracket said, "Well, so be it, we got to move easy." He turned to Johnny. "Son, the gal they might have in yonder. You aimin' to marry her?"

"I am."

The other Brackets exchanged relieved glances.

"Why? What's eatin' you all?" Johnny asked.

"A whore-lady got kilt back in town," said Joe gently.

"Susan Carter!"

"That was her name. Madame Victoria said she had give you a hand. Madame said this Field fella kilt her."

Johnny said, "Yes, I see." He shook his head hard. It was just another score against Morg Field, but he couldn't shake off the memory of quiet desperation in the eyes of the girl, the exhaustion of her voice, the beauty that might have been so valuable, so warm.

Joe Bracket said, "Too bad he's got your gal in there."

"We could sort of teach him not to be killin' people," Sam said thoughtfully. "Specially handsome ladies."

"You better get going," Toole said. "We'll move in, maybe parley with them a little bit."

"Don't start anything," Johnny commanded. "And all of you mind . . . Morg Field belongs to me, personal."

"Well, son, remember you got to catch a fish 'fore you can fry it," said Joe Bracket.

"Don't make any trouble until you hear from me," Johnny insisted. "I want to get back of them, then you can move."

"All right. It's your war, son. We'll just spread out and wait. Give us that hooty owl sign."

"Twice," said Johnny. "Two hooty owls."

He padded away, Monty following closely. Joe Bracket looked at his two elder sons in the moonlight. "Better do like he says, boys. Just get in as close as possible."

"If it only wasn't for the gal, in there," Sam repeated, sighing. "I don't like this kind of dickerin' with fellas like this Field."

Monty made the rope fast to an outcropping stem of rock. Johnny took off his boots. He would have to leave his rifle behind, but he could manage two revolvers, one stuck into his waistband, discarding the unwieldy cartridge belt.

Monty said, "I'll pay it out, so that we do not have friction. Be quite careful about that. Walk the cliffside, do y'understand?"

"I get it," said Johnny. He was impatient to get down there in the back yard where he knew his way out. He said, "Now that Pa and the boys got the front, we're even with 'em. Even if he's got Mary."

"You know he has her," admonished Monty. "Make no doubt. You must act knowing that he has her."

"Okay. Here I go."

He wound the rope around his wrist and began backing down. Many a time he had looked up from labor and admired the brown sheer lift of the bluff behind the ranch. Now it was cold and rough to the touch. He felt it with his feet, the wool sox protecting him but giving warning of sharp edges which could cut the rope and drop him into the midst of danger.

He hoped Monty would have the strength to support him, hurrying a little, anxious to get to the business in hand. He went down, down. The moon picked him up and then he was suddenly aware that anyone glancing upward might see him. He would be an excellent target, spider-like, there against the bluff.

His fear for Mary and his rage against Morg Field stood him well. He eased down below rooftop—that was the barn they had repaired. He felt his feet touch something—it was a pile of rails they had left over from the corral building.

He swung wide from the rails lest they roll loose and give him away. He slacked off the rope, gave it a shake, saw it dangle against the base of the cliff. He waited for Monty to haul it back up.

After a moment he knew the Britisher had no idea of recovering the rope. He was coming down, hand over hand. He was risking everything Johnny had not risked to get into it, where he might do some good.

Johnny went around the corner of the barn. Crouching in shadows he saw the guard, Spud, rifle sloped, yawning, lounging. It was not difficult to get behind the man. He took a revolver from his belt, swung it hard, caught the man around the neck to stifle a yell which did not come. He gagged the man with his own neckerchief, bound him with baling wire, coiled on a hook inside the barn, placed there by Monty's thrifty hand.

Then he cupped his hands and twice gave forth the lonely little cry of the hoot owl. When he heard the answer from across the road Monty had arrived and was kneeling beside him, holding one of the rifles, and how he had brought it down with him Johnny could not imagine.

There was no time to speculate, a gun flashed out front and a voice yelled out, "Field! I'm comin' after you."

The voice sounded a great deal like Johnny's voice. Monty muttered, "I say, that's clever," and Johnny motioned him to quiet, knowing it was his mocking father who called.

There was a pounding of feet and another shot, then a door slammed, the front door. Then a man moaned in pain. That would be the road guard, the man called Eggers. The Brackets did not miss.

Field roared back at them, "Make another move and Mary will die."

"Touch her and you'll live long enough to wish you hadn't," Joe Bracket trumpeted.

"I want to get out," Field answered, obviously well prepared to make his proposition. "I want a free start. She goes with me. When I turn her loose, you can come and get her at a specified place."

There was a silence, then Joe Bracket said, as though uncertain, "Leave us talk it over."

"Make up your mind fast. I haven't got time to palaver," Field said, gaining confidence. "Remember, I got Lonely Jones in here, too."

Johnny whispered, "You stay here. You'll know what to do when the time comes. I'm going in."

"In the house?"

"If the good Lord is willing," said Johnny grimly.

"You'll be killed."

"Maybe. But Pa and the boys will finish it for me."

He was gone in his stockinged feet around the corner of the house. He appreciated every card in Field's hand. He knew stalemate when he encountered it. He also knew that Joe and his brothers were aware of every facet of the deadlock, would anticipate his procedure.

He went directly to the bedroom window. He saw Mary on the bed. He removed his hat, taking a long, careful look at her. She seemed unharmed.

Through the door into the parlor he could see Field. Shade had two revolvers in his hands and was facing the front door. Halliday and Frey were not in sight. He pried with the back of his knife blade at the window and it raised without sound, a tribute to Monty's workmanship.

He heard Shade say, "They might be gettin' closer."

"Not them, not while we got the girl."

Shade said, "I wonder how many there are. If he was alone, it would be a cinch to spread out and rush him."

"He's already got Spud and Eggers," said Field. "He can't be alone. Monty, at least, maybe a couple of those greasers from town."

"I'd like to rush him," said Shade.

"No. He'll give in." Field had not drawn a gun as yet. He seemed supremely confident. He had placed the saddlebags within convenient reach, prepared for leave-taking.

Johnny raised the window halfway under cover of the dialogue in the parlor.

Mary saw him then and as he admonished her to silence their eyes met and caught. He crouched at the window staring at her, realizing what it meant to see her safe, now, at last. He knew it was worth it, he knew that whatever happened in the next few moments, this was his destiny, this was what it all meant, this was his life.

He drew himself up and came feet first over the sill and into the room. He drew the revolvers. He was not a left-handed shooter, but he might need ten shots, he thought, and if they did not get him quickly he could use the second gun on them.

He slid silently across the room. Monty was on the other side of the house. He did not fear Holliday nor Frey. He only wondered how close Joe and the boys had come by now.

Not that it mattered if he could kill in cold blood. They had not seen him, he stood there, guns ready. He had only to open fire and then the family and Monty would come in and that would be the end of it.

Yet he could not. Mary was staring at him, he glanced once her way, then back toward the room. Lonely was lying near the fire, tied to the chair, in sharp pain. The two killers were watching the front as though hypnotized, waiting to hear the answer to their demands.

He aimed at Shade, then lowered the gun. For a long, agonized moment he hesitated, a mark for them if they turned, two against him.

Then he found voice and roared like a clap of thunder, "All right, Field, here's your answer."

As they turned he fired offhand at Shade, because the revolvers were naked in the man's hands. Then he turned upon Field.

But in that precise instant the door slammed open to admit the three Brackets, and from the rear shots sounded and he could hear Frey and Halliday crying in pain or crying quits, out of it one way or the other.

Field had not drawn. He stood, transfixed, even now his eye going to the saddlebags where lay the loot of the town he had thought to bring to his heel.

Then Johnny was across the room, all restraint gone, all rage boiling over, his hands tearing at Field, swinging him, hitting him. The big man fought back automatically and they went around and around the damaged room. Monty came in and held his rifle steady and did not speak. Joe Bracket and the two boys fanned out, dragging Shade's body aside as with ready knives they slashed loose the bindings that held Lonely, lifting him gently, helping him out of harm's way while the fight raged.

In the bedroom Mary looked up into the harsh, kindly face of Joe Bracket and said, "Thank you," when he cut her free, and added, "Is Johnny all right?"

"Why, Miss, mebbe you ought to see for yourself," said Joe and lifted her, supporting her to the parlor door.

Sam and Toole were absorbed. Monty's eyes were dark,

brooding, watching. Field was larger, stronger and in better condition, all knew very well.

Yet there could only be one ending. Johnny hit him hard and full, once, twice, then accepted a blow to the jaw which spun him. Field, knowing all was lost, nonetheless tried hard, his strength was evident.

Johnny went back, no attempt at skill, punching, punishing, revolvers discarded and forgotten. He nailed Field to the wall with his left hand, reached back his right, wanting to do it this way, to punish for Susan Carter, for all the others. His swinging smash plastered Field's nose against one cheek, the next wallop laid him on the floor now so scarred with spur marks.

Field did not stir. Johnny breathed through his mouth, aching, staring down at him.

"He'll hang. I wanted him alive, so that he could hang."

"Yeah," said Joe Bracket. "He'll hang, all right. But you better get over there and hang onto your gal."

Then he looked at her again. She said, "I'm glad you didn't shoot them without warning, Johnny."

"The dang fool," said Joe. Yet he grinned as his youngest son went to the girl and took her in his arms. He closed the bedroom door upon them and nodded brightly to the others.

"Cleanin' up time. Best to give them awhile together whilst we tidy up this here nice house Johnny made."

# chapter fifteen

MAYOR SIME JARRET gave the after-wedding dinner attended by nearly everyone in town excepting Jacob "Morgan" Field, who was safe in the jail with Frey and Halliday squealing against him by the hour. It was held in the cantina, now owned by the widow, Consuela Armindez, at special behest of the groom.

It had been hectic, especially the financial affairs of the bank. Field, alive, owned the bank. That he was accused and patently guilty of looting it, that Frey and Halliday had admitted to robbing Johnny of his eight thousand dollars was gratifying, but there was the matter of financing the mines, of reassuring and repaying investors and depositors.

There had been men from Territorial City and a United States Marshal fortunately known to Sam and Toole. There had been some muddled furor and then Joe Bracket had sent a telegram to El Paso and in return received assurance that anything he needed up to a couple of hundred thousand was immediately available.

That had settled it, so that now all was serene. Joe's sons had been at first amazed, then thoughtful when his wealth was divulged. Joe had been stubbornly silent.

Now, all toasts having been disposed of and the bride blushing prettily at the heaping of compliments upon her beauty, the Mayor arose and spoke.

"I'm real new at this . . ."

Someone said, "G'wan, you never shut up in your life long enough to shave a man."

"I mean this job," said Sime injuredly. "Now, listen to me. I got an idea."

"Hang onto it, you'll never get another," said the heckler, a small man slightly drunken. There was a pause while Sam picked him up and gently threw him out.

"What I mean is, here we got a town. It has already been voted to rename it like it was. Hope City."

There was applause and Lonely Jones wiped a hand over eyes suddenly misty.

Sime went on, "I think we got a good town. We're gathered here, which proves every citizen has got a vote. I expect to be kept in line by the people. That's fine, because like I say, I'm ignorant of the job I got. But I would like to make a strong plea here and now."

He paused and took a long tug at a flagon of Armindez wine, the California kind. Johnny held Mary's hand and wished they would get it over with. Monty had refurbished the house so that it was even prettier than before. He wanted desperately to be alone there with Mary.

Sime said, "Here's what I propose: Joe Bracket should take over the bank. Sam Bracket should resign from his job at Farwell and take over as Marshal here. Toole Bracket should establish headquarters here as representative of the town's interests in the mines, the cattle business and all that there. What do you say, folks?"

There was a concerted roar of approval. Johnny looked at his father and brothers. They were, he saw, affected. He felt a sudden emptiness. Then Joe arose, dressed in a new black suit, wearing a white shirt. He was, Johnny realized, an imposing old rascal. A man could be proud of a father like Joe . . . sometimes.

"That's a very swell speech," said Joe. "Me, personal, I am glad to do anything at all for Hope City. When things get straightened out, I won't need to do anything, because you got all you need without me."

Cries of, "No, we want you . . . We need you . . ." went unheeded. Joe raised his hard, brown hand.

"Speakin' for me and my two sons, I got to tell yawl good people somethin'. We got to refuse your kind and generous offer."

Johnny sighed with relief. He exchanged sly glances with his father, grinned at his brothers.

Sime Jarret said injuredly, "But Joe, can I ask why?"

"I was goin' to tell you." Joe paused for effect, got complete silence. "Us Brackets, we're a strange bunch. Tread on one of us, you got us all to buck. But truth to tell, among ourselves . . ." Again he paused. Then he said flatly, "Truth to tell there just ain't room for all of us in one place." He finished with a rush, "Why, hell, us Brackets, we're bigger'n Texas!"

Johnny led the applause. Then he stood up, his decision firm. He said, "Pa's right. Furthermore, I got enough of listenin' to you folks yap about the town. Mary and me, we got a ranch. Thanks for everything—and you'll excuse us, please."

He grabbed Mary's hand and aimed her at the door. They ran amidst thrown rice and Spanish prayers. They climbed into the carriage made ready and waiting by Monty, who accepted Mary's kiss and waved them on.

They drove through town, past Madame Victoria's and saw the tall woman and Mona and the thin gambler in the window waving to them. They drove past Amsy Buchanan's livery stable and remembered that he had paid too big a price along with Pedro to preserve a town.

Then they thought together that Mary's father had built

upon a dream, even as Johnny Bracket, and now the dream had come true. They drove under the new sign,

HOPE CITY, pop. 2,000

and so to the ranch made clean and comfortable by hands which scrubbed away harsh memories of the past.

**THE END**